The Escape of
Princess Madeline

Kirstin Pulioff

DEDICATION

Dedicated with love to my family.
To Chris, my very own knight in shining armor… and
Adeline & Tommy, who remind me to dream big.

.

CONTENTS

PROLOGUE

King Theodore jumped from his bed. Beads of sweat slid down his temples as his heart threatened to beat out of his chest. Howling wind forced its way into his chamber, extinguishing the dim candlelight.

Braving the cool stones of the castle floor, he walked to the windows at the far end of his chamber. A soft tendril of smoke danced above the blown-out candles. Relighting them, he watched the orange flames flicker in the wind.

Now awake, he leaned over the windowsill, peering into the courtyard below. Small flecks of glittering light reflected off the garden's fountains. Around it, dark cobblestones curved, disappearing into the growing shadows. Nothing stirred in the darkness.

Looking past the courtyard, beyond the castle walls toward the eastern mountains, he watched the rolling hills disappear under a wave of fog. He let out a great sigh, wishing memories could fade the same way.

He wrapped his velvet robe tighter as the wind blew against his face. As his eyes sought clarity from the outside, his mind wandered back to the nightmare that plagued him. Every year on the eve of his children's birthday, King Theodore relived the same dream.

The warm summer breeze and the horn's song greeted him as he stood at the window. A stream of royal visitors and merchants lined the rolling hillsides on their journey to Soron. In anticipation of the summer tournaments and royal births, attendance doubled, bursting the seams of the small kingdom. Peering into the courtyard below, he watched the frenzy with a sad smile. Under colorful banners, people ran back and forth, carrying bundles of fabric, bouquets of wildflowers, and piles of farm produce. The smells of freshly-baked breads and pastries wafted up to him, mixing with the spicy blend of the wizards' incense.

A soft tap on the shoulder brought him back to the room.

"My King," the wizard Elias whispered. "There's nothing more we can do for her. The queen has passed beyond the grasping hands of our magic." King Theodore's heart dropped. The room filled with sage and sandalwood spun as he looked at the group of wizards surrounding the bed. Stumbling forward, he dropped to his knees, cradling Eleanor's pale hand in his. With a heave, he wept, burying his tear-stained face in his hands.

"We knew this day was coming, my lord," Elias said, sharing a look of concern with the other wizards. "The mirror warned that a sacrifice was necessary to protect the kingdom. She died for you. Giving her life to bring you these wonderful children and save…" Elias stopped as his eyes connected with the king's.

Tears froze on King Theodore's face. His jaw clenched at the wizard's words. "She did this for me?" the king bellowed, heat rising in his cheeks. "She sacrificed herself and left me alone for my benefit? How dare you! This was your failure, not her sacrifice!"

King Theodore stood and looked the older wizard in the eyes. His face matched the red of his velvet robe. "Hear my words, great wizard. This will not go unpunished."

Waving his arms abruptly, he ushered them out, shutting the door in haste behind them. He approached the queen. His body *shook as new tears rolled down his cheeks. He wept until the golden light from the windows faded, his fingers lingering on Eleanor's silk gown.*

The morning sun rose over the horizon, streaking the countryside with an orange and red wave. King Theodore didn't notice this beauty—or any beauty. Sitting calmly in his throne, he watched as the room filled with visitors. His face, like stone, refused to give way, noticing but not reacting to the growing crowd, or their sympathies.

With weary eyes and a tight jaw, he looked over the room. Faces painted with anticipation, fear, and curiosity stared back at him. No one had expected him this morning. He barked an order to a nearby steward, breaking the silence.

The steward's eyes bulged as King Theodore delivered his message. With a curt nod of approval, the steward lifted his horn to his lips, announcing the royal decree.

The horn echoed off the stained glass windows crowning the throne room. The gathered crowd quieted, looking at the steward expectantly. The knights stood straight against the side wall, and the wizards folded their arms inside their robes.

"By royal decree," the steward's voice croaked, "the services of the wizards are no longer needed or approved of in this kingdom." The uproar of the room overpowered his weak voice. The other wizards leaned in toward their leader, Elias, with questioning looks. Elias refused to break eye contact with the king.

With another nod, the king encouraged the steward to continue. A small smile broke the severity of the king's face as he heard his orders proclaimed. "By reason of treason, you are to be punished with death." The steward hung his head with the last words.

A shocked gasp ran through the hall. With a wave of his arm, the king directed the knights into position around the unarmed men.

Elias tightened his lips and kneeled before the throne. "My lord, please reconsider these actions. It is not our fault. You must know that."

Every head turned to the king.

King Theodore stood, amplifying his authority. "I thought the proclamation was simple to understand. You said it yourself, you knew of the tragedy before it happened." Taking slow steps toward Elias, he continued. "You saw this coming—the death of my wife, your queen—and you did nothing. With all your power and foresight, you did nothing to stop this atrocity. That alone is punishable by death."

The king hesitated at the depth of grief in Elias's eyes. "However, you are my beloved's kinsmen, and so I shall save you. Exile is generous. You're to leave by day's end. Be warned, if you so much as enter the kingdom or whisper its name, your protection will be gone, and I will not stop my men from killing you."

King Theodore stormed out amidst a confused uproar of questions.

The next sound King Theodore heard pulled at his heart. Outside the royal nursery, his hands stayed on the steel handle.

The nurse opened the door, cradling a baby in each arm. "Your Majesty," she cried, exasperated. "The children, they cry for you."

"No," he answered, looking down at the woman, "they cry for their mother."

The wind shrieked through the window, blowing out the candles once more. King Theodore let the darkness hide his tears.

"My Eleanor, sixteen years have passed, and the children and I still grieve for you as if it were yesterday," King Theodore whispered into the night.

CHAPTER ONE

"Father, this is beautiful!" Madeline squealed. A thrill ran through her as she felt the smooth bumps of the pearls and traced the golden embroidery. "I have to try this on!" she yelled, running into the other room.

Looking down at the dress, a wave of wonder rolled over her. Her father's gifts, although generous, never surprised her. There had been a pony for her fifth birthday, but 'Princess' had only lasted a few months. After tossing Madeline and breaking her arm, 'Princess' was also tossed. After that, gifts of books, embroidery, and music became normal.

This year was different. This dress was different. Effortlessly, the green silk gown slipped up and over her head. She smiled at her image in the mirror. Never before had she looked so beautiful. Clinging to her new curves, the dress fit perfectly. Above the decorated bodice, her long, dark brown hair shimmered against the pale green silk. The gown was a shade lighter than her eyes and highlighted their beauty and depth. A smile filled her face as she marveled at the woman staring back at her.

Remembering her father in the other room, she pried her eyes away from her reflection and peeked around the corner. Sitting in her oversized plush chair, he looked out of place. His dark crimson robe clashed with the soft pastels and golden hues of the room. Entangled in a pile of floral pillows, soft dolls, and half-finished embroidery projects, King Theodore kept his head low, twisting his fingers. Tears welled up as she recognized a rare moment of nervousness.

He looked up as she twirled around the corner. "How does it fit?" he asked eagerly, a smile stretched across his face.

"Oh, Father, it's wonderful!" she exclaimed, spinning into his arms.

"My princess," he said, "you look beautiful."

Madeline stepped back and twirled into a curtsey, showing the full effect of the gown. "Do you like it?" she asked.

"Darling, I love it, and I love you. Happy birthday. You'll capture everyone's eyes and hearts this evening at the ball." He squeezed her hands and smiled. Madeline's heart soared at the pride twinkling in his eyes.

She had noticed the frenzied stewards running in and out of the grand hall with food, decorations, fresh flowers, and music the past week, but hadn't given them a second thought. Decorated in the same fashion for years, the ball—and every other event—remained predictable.

Royal balls captured the hearts of everyone in Soron, everyone but Madeline. The years of duty, hiding behind poise and manners, wore on her. As she looked at her new gown and felt the smooth fabric over her skin, she hoped this year might be different. New visions played in her mind.

"I hardly think anyone will pay me too much attention," she said.

Her father gave her a mischievous smile and a wink.

"Of course they will. This is more than our annual summer ball. Tonight, the ball is in your honor, for your betrothal."

Princess Madeline's mouth dropped open. The playful smile on her father's face contradicted every emotion running through her.

"What?" she asked in a whisper, hoping she had heard wrong. She sat down and clutched a floral pillow to her stomach. Anger and confusion boiled within. Her head shook with disbelief. "It can't be time for that already."

Her father raised his eyebrows, surprised at her reaction. "It's your sixteenth birthday, my dear. It's time, and furthermore, it's your duty."

She threw the pillow at her father and bit her lower lip at his scowl. "I'm not ready to be married. What about Braden instead? He'll happily do his duty." She refused to meet his eyes.

"Young lady, do not scoff at the importance of duty. This is not about you."

"Not about me? You're talking about my future, my marriage!"

He tightened his jaw and handed her back her pillow. "I am talking about the future of Soron, and peace within the territories. It's our duty to continue our traditions, at whatever cost. We provide the structure, routines, and leadership for the entire realm. That comes with expectations for all of us." He gave her a pointed look. "Now, I don't want to hear any more pouting."

"I won't marry them," she mumbled.

"Yes, daughter, you will. All these men come from royal backgrounds, and marrying you is a high honor.

You're of marrying age and will carry out your duties. That is final," he said. His face darkened as he shut the door behind him.

Princess Madeline bowed over in her chair, her face in her hands. Feelings of betrayal settled in her as she looked down at the beautiful gown. A tear slid down her cheek, darkening the fabric as it soaked into the golden threads.

Her insides twisted with anger and anguish as her dreams of adventure evaporated. In times like this, she couldn't help but wonder if things would have been different if her mother were still alive.

Trapped under the unrelenting rules of her father, at times she felt more like a damsel in distress than a princess. She always thought there would be more time. More time to dream, to explore, and to be free from rules and responsibilities.

The sun shone through the window, sparkling off the golden embroidery and drying the tear drops. The noise from the courtyard below brought her to the windowsill. Leaning over, she watched the people run from one side of the courtyard to the other. Farmers with bundles, musicians, kids holding wooden swords, women in their flowing gowns, all strolled cheerfully below. Her face grew hotter by the minute—from the sun and from jealousy. The carefree laughter, birds singing, music playing. It sounded dull to her. Nothing brightened her shadow of disappointment.

"How can I make him understand?" she asked, leaning against the stone window. The warm breeze blew against her, brushing her hair off her shoulders and bringing a new sound. Madeline squinted, concentrating on the high-pitched giggle, and smiled.

"That's it," she declared, running out the door. "Sophia can help me."

Madeline and Sophia had been best friends since they were little. Playing in the nursery, riding ponies, sharing secret handshakes and hideouts, they had been inseparable. They didn't even need to talk—sometimes a quick glance or gesture was all it took to drive the other to laughter or tears. Though in the past few years, as the differences in their royal ranks became more apparent and new priorities emerged, a gap had formed. At the core, they were still best friends, but currently they only shared one thing— Madeline's brother.

She darted down the stairs and out the door, apologizing as she bumped into an elderly steward. Stacks of books flew out of his arms, landing with a thud on the stone floor. His annoyance didn't stop her from scurrying off behind the busy line of attendants.

Gray corridors intertwined and curved. She ran past the empty library and slowed by the kitchen, taking in the lingering smell of rosemary and ham. Her path to the courtyard stalled in the common room that overflowed with visiting royalty. Constant chatter filled the room as knights, lords, and duchesses conversed over the portraits and tapestries. Housing one of the largest collections of historical art, the walls of Soron came alive with their history, triumphs, and legends. Slowing her pace, she nodded to her favorite duchess before scurrying outside.

- *Kirstin Pulioff* -

Bursting into the courtyard, Princess Madeline smiled at the commotion. Despite her earlier feelings, the merriment was contagious. Music surrounded her as she twisted her way through the crowd. She pressed against the farmers and merchants, careful to lift the hem of her gown. Opposition to her father's plan didn't mean risking her beautiful new dress. As the crowd cleared, she saw her friend.

Sitting on the edge of the fountain, underneath the marble archway, Sophia's red hair sparkled in the sunlight. Her familiar laugh rose above the others.

Madeline stopped as a new figure popped into view. She groaned as her brother leaned in for a kiss.

She felt heat rise to her cheeks, and coughed as she moved forward. Trying to be loud and obvious, she stomped across the cobblestones. Braden's green eyes shot open and he laughed deeply.

"Madeline," he said, as if she hadn't interrupted. "Happy birthday." He brushed his dark hair back and smoothed the front of his shirt.

"Happy birthday," she mumbled back, feeling awkward at her intrusion.

"Oh, Princess Madeline," Sophia said. "You surprised us."

"It looks like I did," she mumbled.

Sophia joined in with a giggle, batting her eyes at Braden.

"You're lucky it was me. You know what father would say," she scolded.

"Father would say what he always does. Braden," he

mimicked in a deep voice, "Good job."

Sophia burst into laughter. Madeline just stared at them. "And yet he wants me to get married. It looks more like this ball should be for you."

"Madeline, relax. It's just a ball. There'll be people from all over, people that will help the kingdom. Think of this as your way to prove yourself a good leader." His smile grated on her. "That's a very pretty dress."

"You know this is not fair." As her agitation spread across her face, his smile grew.

"Aw, Madeline, don't get mad. You know this is how it goes."

"It shouldn't have to. I should have every right to live my life, like you, or Sophia, or anyone else in this kingdom."

Sophia's smile disappeared. "Not everyone has the choices that you think they do. You should be happy about all the men you'll get to choose from. Not all of us get what we want." Her voice held an edge.

Madeline looked at them, flustered. This wasn't going the way she intended. "Sophia, I need your help. I can't go through with this."

"It's your duty." Sophia said. "You must."

"You can't be serious," she said, searching her friend's face for a hint of support. "You've always helped me."

"I know, but…" Sophia's voice trailed off, and her eyes refocused on Braden. "Some things change."

Looking at Sophia and her brother, she realized her two dearest friends wouldn't help. She didn't even bother saying goodbye to them; they were already back doing what she had interrupted.

Madeline climbed the stairs back to her room and slammed the door shut. She threw her pillows against the far wall until a small garden of roses and pastels grew up to the window. She fumed for a few minutes before deciding on a plan.

Maybe they were right. It was her duty to be at the ball tonight, but that didn't mean she had to cooperate with the marriage.

"Time to get ready," she said, taking one last look at herself in the mirror.

CHAPTER TWO

Sunsets in Soron were a sight to see. The way the colors ignited the sky, reds, oranges, and yellows, made it look as if the sunlight melted into darkness. Beauty reflected off the clouds, amplifying every color. At sunset, King Theodore planned for that warmth and beauty to set fire to the ballroom.

A row of knights lined the castle walls, shining beneath the torches, directing visitors to the grand ballroom. The richness and prestige of the kingdom surrounded their path. Golden banners marked with the red dragon of Soron soared overhead. A slow melody filled the background as guests arrived.

Decorated to match the sunset, the ballroom shimmered with red and orange banners. A soft breeze floated through the room, rustling the flags, making the colors dance. Yellow and white roses decorated the tables, invigorating the senses as their sweet aroma floated through the air.

King Theodore walked about the ballroom, appraising the gathering crowd. Royalty from the north and prominent merchants from the west and south intermixed with his villagers. The room overflowed with possibilities.

Nodding to several people, he pressed his way through the thickening crowd on his way to the front stairs. His smile grew in anticipation. Surely one of these men would win over his daughter.

He raised his glass of wine above his head and addressed his guests.

"Ladies and gentlemen, thank you all for coming this evening." He cleared his throat and looked around. "I know you have traveled a great distance, and I assure you, it was worth it." A light chuckle broke out as he continued.

"It is my great pleasure to welcome you to the Kingdom of Soron, and to this royal ball celebrating Princess Madeline's birthday and betrothal. As a child, she dreamed of adventure. Alas, ruling a kingdom does not allow much time for adventures. So, I must entrust that to one of you. Tonight, it's my hope that someone will win her heart. That one of you will join the Kingdom of Soron for a prosperous future, provide for my daughter, and give her the adventure she has dreamed of."

He watched the eligible men crowd at the base of the stairs, waiting for her entrance. Their etiquette disappeared as they strove for the first advantage, fighting amongst themselves for a better position.

King Theodore raised his hand for silence.

"It is my pleasure to introduce my daughter, the rose of our valley, the fire in our sunsets, our beautiful Princess Madeline." The crowd roared as they waited for her entrance. Trumpets burst into action with an escalating fanfare.

Bringing his glass to his lips, he savored the sweet taste. His eyes twinkled with hope.

***

Butterflies stampeded around in her stomach as Madeline paced the hallway. Proper entrance protocol required that she wait until the formal introductions ended. Until then, she had no choice but to worry behind a velvet curtain about her father's intentions.

One of her father's personal attendants guarded her path. She knew this by the royal crest, a golden dragon, sewn onto the steward's tunic. He had never sent one of his personal attendants before. She wondered about the extra security, until she remembered their earlier argument. A smile flickered on her lips. Maybe he had reason to be concerned about her behavior.

"It's almost time, Princess," the steward said, giving her a smile.

She returned his smile with one of her rehearsed ones, hiding her fears behind a wall of formality.

The trumpets sounded and, slowly, the man pulled the curtain to the side, creating a small path for her. It was time. She ran the back of her hands across her forehead and fluffed her hair before walking through.

The curtain swished behind her, closing the path and the quickest route back to her chambers. She took a deep breath and closed her eyes.

"I can do this," she said to herself. "This is no different than every other year. Father wouldn't make me marry someone I didn't know."

A trace of doubt lingered beneath her smile as she turned the final corner. She smiled amidst the resounding cheers but felt their silent scrutiny. Every person watched, appraising her smallest step.

The cool handrail of the marble staircase took her back to her first royal ball. As a small girl of only five, the first time she walked down the long staircase, she could hardly reach the handrail and her chin quivered to the point of tears. Over the years, new feelings surfaced, turning the quivering chin into a smile. For one moment, on that staircase, she felt unmatched. In her slow descent, nothing took precedence over her in her father's eyes.

This year, she didn't want that attention. She wanted nothing more than to run back up the stairs and hide in her room like a little girl. Like at that first ball, a fear of the unknown weighed her down.

When she cleared the stairs, a throng of people collapsed in on her. Ogling eyes raked over her and presumptive hands grabbed her arms. Her heart pounded as her personal space disappeared.

"There will be time for everyone," her father laughed, taking his position at her side. "There's no need to crowd. Princess Madeline is excited to meet you all."

Her father's reassurance warmed her, until she looked up and saw his expression. To the unstudied eye, her father looked composed. But she knew the truth. Years of provoking him and dealing with the aftermath had made her an expert at discerning his emotions from the fine lines of his face. A furrowed brow for worry and concern, a twinkle in his eyes and slightly flared nostrils for happiness, and, most important, the flinty stare and the smile with only one dimple for the moments that he couldn't express his rage.

In that moment, when her eyes connected with her father's, she saw his unbalanced smile. She had changed into a new gown. It was still beautiful, just different from his expectation. The ivory dress featured delicate rose accents and velvet trim. Its contrasting colors looked striking against her pale skin and dark hair. Curled and pinned on top of her head, her hairdo allowed a few loose strands to cascade down her back and frame her face. Her eyes twinkled with the secret disobedience.

Triumph washed over her, and she met his strong gaze with her own.

"Father," she said with a deep curtsey. Holding her pose, she waited for him to take her hand.

"Good evening, Princess," he said as he reached forward.

Any advantage she felt disappeared. His dimple disappeared under a smirk, and she knew he had a new plan.

King Theodore led her to the center of the ballroom. The crowd looked on, oblivious to the tension between them. Plastered smiles stayed on their faces as they prepared for the dance. A smooth, almost hypnotic melody started and they raised their arms over their heads for the first pose.

Traditionally shared between the king and queen, the first dance marked a special moment for Madeline and her father. At her first royal ball, to stop her quivering chin and keep the tears from falling down her face, King Theodore had wrapped her in his arms and danced.

The tradition had continued, although tonight their

dance was spoiled under the duplicity of formality for the guests and the intensity of her defiance.

"I don't understand why you're doing this, Madeline." Her father commented as she twirled under his arm. "I was very specific about that dress this morning. This one is beautiful, but it is not what I wanted."

Madeline forced her smile a bit more and looked down. "Really?" she asked innocently. "I thought this was perfect for the evening. This is my best color and will bring me a higher bidding price." She rolled her eyes as she moved behind her father's back.

The melody continued, its emotive beauty lost on them both. King Theodore twirled her in the detailed steps of the dance.

"This is no way," he started, "for you to behave." Twirl and bow. "Or appear." Step, step, and bend. "That dress was important to me; you should be wearing it." Twirl, side step, twirl. The tempo increased, matching the speed of the quips in their argument.

"Father, don't be silly," she said, slightly out of breath. "It's just a dress. I can wear it next time, in a few years, when I'm ready to be married."

"That's not up for discussion. It's part of your duties," he countered. "Changing a dress will not change my mind."

"I will not sit down and let you decide whom I marry and what I wear." Her jaw hurt from clenching. "This is my life." She twirled with a grand flourish and curtsied toward her father. "This is my choice." Feeling all eyes on her, she blushed under the scrutiny of her admirers and the cold glare of her father.

The crowd clapped as the dance ended and a new one began. Many couples joined the dance floor, and Madeline fled to the far end of the ballroom.

Looking over her shoulder, she saw a group of men encircle her father. A mixture of relief and dread rolled over her. She had escaped for a moment, but she knew the evening was just beginning. Searching the crowd, she hoped to find Sophia, but her eyes got lost in a sea of colors as people danced to the music.

Madeline walked around, taking inventory. The dim light hid the faces in the overcrowded hall. She saw some familiar people—princes, kings, and other royalty that had done business with their kingdom. Older and grayer than before, but a welcome sight in a hall filled with unfamiliar faces. Every way she turned, a bevy of strangers smiled at her.

She stopped against the back wall to catch her breath. The constant winks unsettled her. Knowing smiles seemed to lurk beneath their gazes. Her face reddened with humiliation, anger, and something else she couldn't place. Not wanting to dwell on that feeling, she looked for a way out.

Guards stood on either side of the entrance doors. Stiff armor gleamed in the candlelight. There was no way out but the way she'd entered. The grand staircase hid behind a throng of suitors.

She relaxed when a familiar face met her gaze. Walking toward her, the Duchess of Mallory held her arms open.

"Princess Madeline," the woman said, embracing her warmly. "What a wonderful ball."

"Thank you for coming this evening," she smiled back, formality surfacing out of reflex. "What a beautiful gown," she said, admiring it. Black velvet draped the older woman's curves, and diamond accents flashed in the dim light. The glimmer reminded her of the golden embroidery on her new green gown. The gown lying in a heap on the floor of her room.

Under the Duchess of Mallory's silver-streaked hair, rosy cheeks and a genuine smile welcomed her. The duchess was the same age her mother would have been. She exuded warmth, and Madeline sank into her arms gratefully.

"Oh, this old gown, you are such a dear," the duchess laughed heartily, leaning in to speak above the music. "I remember my sweet sixteenth. Ah, it seems just like yesterday." A content smile played on her lips.

"It must have been wonderful," Madeline encouraged her.

"Oh, it was…"

Madeline smiled and waited for more, but the duchess didn't continue. Worried she might lose her attention, Madeline tried again. "What happened at yours?"

"Oh, I'm sorry," the duchess apologized, patting her chest. "I sometimes get lost in my own place." She continued when Madeline smiled. "At my sweet sixteen, I met my beloved Thomas." She winked at her. "This is a great opportunity."

Madeline cringed. The duchess looked her over

appraisingly. Her gaze was almost worse than the looks the men had given her.

"I haven't seen you in this dress before," she said, patting her on the shoulder. "You're beautiful, just like your mother."

Madeline unconsciously ran her fingers over the ruffled roses on her dress, hoping her face wasn't nearly as red as it felt. "Thank you," she murmured, keeping her eyes lowered. Leaning into the older woman, Madeline looked up, sincerity in her eyes. "You knew Lord Thomas before you married, though—you loved him, right?"

"Well," the duchess whispered back, "you never really know someone until you marry them. Thomas and I were introduced that night, arrangements were made, and we fell in love after we were married." Her gaze drifted off in a memory and refocused across the room, on King Theodore.

"I see your father coming. With a prince," she added. "I will leave you for a short while. Have fun!" She smiled and walked off, leaving Madeline alone.

Madeline turned around, facing the wall, hoping that if she couldn't see them, then they couldn't see her. She cringed and forced a smile when she felt a tap on her shoulder.

"Princess Madeline," her father announced. "Please meet our neighbor to the north, Prince Alleg."

She almost laughed when she saw the man standing beside her father. Her eyes grew with disbelief as she counted the deep lines crossing his face. The years in the harsh sun had not been kind to the prince. This had to be a joke on her father's part. He couldn't possibly want her wed to a man older than himself.

"Prince Alleg, it's nice to meet you." She hid her disdain in a curtsey. "On a clear day, I can see the Dragon's Gate arch from our library. Is it as beautiful in person as it is from afar?"

"It is beautiful, but not nearly as beautiful as you." His dry lips scraped over her hands as he lifted them in a kiss. "I would be honored to show you it one day. The beauty of the north is different than here in the inland. There is much to enjoy—exotic spices, rare jewels, rich weavers..." His words trailed off.

King Theodore excused himself as the prince continued.

She pleaded with her eyes, but he ignored her. A small smirk played on his lips. She sighed as he disappeared into the crowd.

Madeline managed a small smile for the prince. A gnawing pain grew in her stomach as she listened to the man, heard the implication of his words. The idea of becoming his wife nauseated her.

Prince Alleg continued speaking, walking her toward the secluded shadows of the room. Her heart pounded as his grip tightened on her elbow.

"We mustn't leave the ball," she panicked, trying to pull him back to the light.

His eyes stared, piercing through her dress. "I thought maybe some privacy would be in order to discuss our wedding." His eyes quickly rolled back over her.

His boldness shocked her. Her heart beat wildly as

she scanned the room for help. Now that she wanted eyes on her, she found none. Draping her right hand over her forehead, she feigned weakness.

"I need a moment, sir," she said, fanning herself with both hands to add space between them. She didn't doubt the pink tone of her face; outrage alone darkened it. "Sir, we must discuss this matter later. I am feeling too faint at the moment." Madeline fluttered her eyelashes for added effect. "I will be back shortly," she said, walking away from him. She had no intention of returning.

The moment of relief didn't last long. Before she got the chance to hide from any new suitors, she saw her father's crimson robe. He approached with a new man cloaked in black. Behind them, she saw the Duchess of Mallory watching with curiosity.

Madeline tried to walk by, but the king grabbed her arm and made her stay.

"Princess Madeline, I wanted to introduce you to a new visitor to the kingdom. This is Prince Paulsen from Morengo, on the southern edges by the sea. He has traveled the farthest to meet you and was hoping for a dance." Her father winked at her and motioned to the band to start a new song.

Prince Paulsen laughed and bowed deep. "Your father seems a bit enthusiastic this evening." Deep blue eyes twinkled at her above a mesmerizing smile.

"That is certainly one word for it," she agreed. He was just a few years older than herself, and she relaxed in his company. Prince Paulsen carried himself with the confidence of a noble: calm, poised, and charming.

"Father said this is your first time here in our kingdom. How do you like it so far?"

"Each moment is better than the last." His words lingered in her ears, and she forgot her reservations.

Time slipped away as they danced. She floated along to the music, guided by Prince Paulsen's lead and strong arms. Behind his shoulder, the Duchess of Mallory watched with a smile, nodding her approval. Prince Paulsen must have passed her test.

Her approval reminded Madeline of the principle of the matter. Her smile faded. Handsome or not, she refused to give in to her father's demands.

"I'm sorry, I really must go," she said, stopping mid-step.

"Go?" he questioned, looking around. "But we're in the middle of a dance."

"I know, but I'm not feeling well."

"I can try to help," he offered with a smile.

"I'm sorry, you must excuse me." She pulled out of his grasp.

"Of course," he said, but she noticed his eyes darken.

The staircase that meant her freedom kept moving. She hadn't noticed how far they had danced until she looked at the stairs, positioned at the far side of the room. Her escape still remained out of reach.

The music continued, and the trumpets blared in a rising crescendo. She moved in rhythm to the music, matching its tempo. Each step took her closer and closer until she felt the cool surface of the handrail. As the trumpets reached their final note and she took the first step up, someone grabbed her hand.

As she turned, her father greeted her disappointment with the next suitor. Her plan had not worked. No matter what she did, he kept bringing men over. What would it take to get him to understand?

Baron Elliot, a quiet, middle-aged man, ran the sheep farms near Morengo. Not royalty, but a wealthy merchant with business interests and extensive trading routes. Crinkling her nose slightly at the lingering smell of sheep mixed with wine, she curtseyed and touched his outstretched hand with her fingertips.

Having had a bit too much to drink, he stumbled into her as he bowed. She shot her father a look of disbelief. King Theodore raised his eyebrows in warning before walking away.

The Baron's words were slurred as he attempted to be charming. His already-strong accent was garbled by wine, and she didn't understand anything he said. His gestures left even more to the imagination. But she understood his eyes. Bulging and red, they raked over her body. His hand slid along the railing at her side until he leaned against her.

Madeline looked at Baron Elliot and bit her lower lip, then gave in and ran up the stairs.

She didn't look back or stop until her bedroom door locked in place behind her. Leaning against the back of her door, she savored the victory. She had made it.

Smiling to herself, she undressed, humming a melody while pulling up the covers. She tucked herself in and smiled, prepared for the sweet dreams of success.

***

King Theodore fumed as Madeline ran up the stairs. Her attitude needed adjusting before people knew of her disobedience. His eyes wandered from potential suitors to the decorations to the dancers, and settled on a guard. An idea filtered in.

He raised his glass to the surrounding crowd.

"It seems," he began with a glance around the room and a deep chuckle, "that the excitement of the evening has caused our Princess to feel faint. I can only hope that a good night's rest will leave her ready for tomorrow's feat. Instead of our normal summer tournament, I suggest we find her a champion. May our Princess have sweet dreams of suitors," he said, winking to the gentlemen. "And may we drink and dance to the celebration at hand."

The room roared with excitement as the band started back up. An upbeat melody left dancers laughing as they spun. Colors twirled like a living rainbow.

King Theodore sipped his glass and smiled. A few unplanned events, but everything still progressed. He had a plan, and it was nothing that a tantrum could stop.

CHAPTER THREE

The morning sunrise burst into the armory, its ruby rays matching the hot coals. A group of knights gathered around the fire pit, putting the finishing touches on their armor. The air was filled with a multitude of sounds— rhythmic ringing as they hammered out dents, the soft scraping of sword against stone, and the hiss of steam as cool water dripped onto hot coals. Discontent rose over the commotion.

The king's enthusiastic announcement about the change in tournament translated into tedious work and an early morning for the knights. It changed today's event from a simple afternoon tournament to an all-day ceremony with a serious prize. That accounted for the majority of the grumbles.

"It'd be one thing if the king had given us notice to prepare," muttered one of the knights, dripping in sweat.

"The king's messenger woke me late last night with the news. That's hardly enough time to get ready or even get most of the bumps out of my breastplate," another knight chimed in as steam hissed around him.

Murmurs of agreement rolled through the small room. The mugginess of the air amplified their agitation.

"What a prize too," the first knight grumbled again. "To win the chance to be the princess's champion and protect her wherever she goes. My loyalty is to the king." He continued sharpening his axe without looking up to see the others nod. Several grunts of agreement sounded from the knights.

"She's not bad, she's just a kid," another said.

"Well, one thing is for sure, whoever wins will be getting a handful." The room burst into laughter.

One knight knelt to the side, refusing to join in the conversation.

Quiet and pensive, Daniel worked in silence. His steel gray eyes focused on his work. He gave this preparation his full attention, the same way he worked on all his tasks. His calloused hands, rough from work in the armory and on the battlefield, polished his shield. He unconsciously blew his sandy blonde hair out of his eyes as the steam and sweat rolled down his forehead. It was Daniel's first tournament; he wanted to win. He felt pressure, not only for himself—he needed to make his family proud.

He carefully lifted his armor. Originally his grandfather's, it had been refitted specifically for him. Their family crest was etched into the shield and breastplate, indicating their lineage, loyalty, and strength. A modified oak tree covered the bottom half, with a sword for its trunk. The top showcased the emblem of the red dragon for the Kingdom of Soron.

The coals from the nearby fire burned red hot. Every once in a while, a blast of steam shot toward him as the hot steel touched the cool water, setting the metal in place. His reflection in the armor winked back at him. Only a few more dents to go, and he would be ready. His mind wandered into memories while he finished the tedious tasks.

Nervousness wracked Daniel's body as he approached the king. His leather boots scuffed the floor, and his sword jingled at his side against the chainmail. He knelt stiffly on the floor in front of the throne. The king must have sensed his apprehension because he smiled down at him with a rich, warm laugh.

The grand hall overflowed. Villagers from Soron and travelers from the nearby territories had come to see the ceremony. Every year, a new batch of apprentices swore their loyalty and devotion to the kingdom, with the hope of becoming a knight. After years of studying, training, and serving, it was his turn. With five other boys from the village, Daniel waited, feeling the eyes and expectations of the crowd. Sparing a quick glance behind him, he saw pride beaming from his parents. His heart beat wildly waiting for the ceremony to begin.

And then he saw her. For the first time, his heart skipped a beat, and the world slowed down.

The king spoke of duty, loyalty, and chivalry, all the sacred rites of knighthood, but Daniel barely heard. The beauty that stood before him mesmerized him.

Standing at the right-hand side of the throne, she held a handful of white roses. Her dark hair contrasted with her ivory gown. A faint smile rested on her lips as she looked over the crowded hall. Poised beneath the focus of the crowd, she represented the image of what they served to protect, a reminder of the innocence of their people and the beauty of their kingdom. Daniel knew, in that moment, he would give his life to protect her.

In a moment quicker than he imagined, the king lifted his sword. The cold steel pressed down on him, and his focus returned to the king and the responsibility attached to his words. A breath later, *the ceremony ended, and the crowd erupted in cheers.*

He felt the congratulatory hugs of his family and the other knights. Above the rising noise and gathering crowd, he lost sight of the princess.

And then the crowds parted and she reappeared, smiling at him. He froze under the spell of her emerald eyes. Princess Madeline walked toward him and handed him a single white rose. The softness of her touch surprised him, as did her whispered words.

"My knight," she whispered before disappearing into the crowd. That marked the start of a new life for him.

Two words, spoken softly, gave him a new direction. They drove him through the hard work and training, healing his bruises and pain. Today he would prove her words true and become her knight.

Lifting his breastplate into position, the warmth of security washed over him. The weight of the armor settled onto his shoulders, putting him at ease. A blast of the trumpets announced the tournament's approach. Daniel moved quickly to join the other knights, staying quiet amidst the cheers and triumphant cries. He was focused and ready.

***

Madeline awoke to Sophia shaking her roughly in her bed.

"Wake up, Princess, you don't have much time," Sophia pleaded, leaning over her.

"A few more minutes," she murmured, pulling the

covers over her head.

Even under the covers, she could not escape the start of the day. Sunshine peeked through the eyelets on her blanket, birds chirped, and Sophia poked her ticklish sides. She may have faked a headache last night, but it was real this morning. The bright sunlight and sharp chirps made her head want to explode.

Sophia snatched the covers and shook her head. "You don't have any more time," she insisted.

Madeline rubbed her eyes before seeing Sophia's scowl. "What?" she asked.

"What?" Sophia repeated incredulously. She paced across the room, tightlipped, her hands on her hips. Madeline, still groggy, felt dizzy watching her friend move. "You have to get ready. They're all waiting for you downstairs," Sophia said, rummaging through the closet.

"Who is waiting, and for what? The tournament doesn't start until this afternoon," Madeline mumbled, truly confused. Yawning, she sat up, watching dresses pile up on the ground and the edge of the chair as Sophia selected and discarded her gowns.

"Plans changed," Sophia sighed, holding a deep blue gown against herself in the mirror. Madeline saw the longing in Sophia's eyes as she stared at her reflection. "After last night, you should be grateful they stayed and are still pursuing you. You missed out on quite the celebration." Sophia shook her head and pushed the blue gown into Madeline's hands. "Here, this is perfect. Now get up, I need to get you ready."

Madeline looked down at the dress and then up at her

friend. "I don't understand what you're talking about." She stood to slip the dress over her head. "I met the men last night and then came back up here. That should be it. I didn't choose any of them." She pulled the dress down and looked over at Sophia, who was staring back at her, her eyebrows raised.

"You are a princess, Madeline. Do you not realize how this works?" Sophia berated her. "Did you honestly think your father would back down so easily? He's been setting this up for months. If you don't choose, he will."

"Do you really think so?" Madeline asked quietly.

"Yes," Sophia said, more softly, moving around to tie the back of the dress. "After you left the ball, your father apologized profusely and announced a change of plans. Instead of the normal summer tournament, today marks the tournament to find your champion. I'm afraid it's not over. Not even remotely."

She took a deep breath and cringed as Sophia tugged on the back of her dress, tightening the bodice.

"Before every princess gets married, she is awarded a knight champion to guard her once she leaves the kingdom. Today, you get yours."

Sophia's harsh words started to sink in. "He still plans to make me marry one of them?" she asked, her voice shaking.

Sophia had lost all her patience at this point, and laid both her hands on Madeline's shoulders.

"Madeline," she said, "you're a princess—our princess. It's your duty. You should be happy that they're all gathered downstairs waiting to escort you to the fairgrounds." Sophia stepped back and looked her over appraisingly.

Madeline numbly watched the evolution of her reflection as she grew more and more presentable. By the end, even she had to admit she looked perfect.

In the mirror, a carefully crafted image stared back at her. Beautiful and poised, she hid her fear and disappointment behind a mask. The only thing missing was a smile. The midnight blue gown Sophia chose fit perfectly. Her pale skin shimmered beneath it.

She winced as her friend wove her hair into a braided crown atop her head. The merciless tugging exasperated her headache. Pain drew her mind away from the gnawing pit in her stomach. She covered her mid-section as she searched Sophia's face.

"Can you think of a way out? I don't think I can do this. I'm just not ready," she pleaded.

"Madeline, what's the big deal? It's just a marriage, not the end of the world." Sophia dropped the brush.

"No, just the end of my freedom."

"Well, at least you have a choice," Sophia snapped.

"You call an old man or a drunken merchant choices? Having a choice implies it's my decision. And, ultimately, it's not."

"I don't know what to tell you," Sophia said, picking the brush back up to finish her hair. "I wished you realized that you're lucky."

She knew by the look on Sophia's face that she was thinking about her own situation.

"It's time to go," Sophia said, setting the brush on the

vanity. "You can do what you will, but I can't disobey the king. And you love tournaments. It will be fun. There'll be knights, jousting, swordplay, banners, the whole works. It can't be that bad."

Sophia dragged her out of the room and led her down the halls. They walked silently through the maze of corridors, passing the red curtain marking the upper entrance to the ballroom. Her mind spun as she gripped the cool handrail and saw the group gathered at the bottom.

Her heart dropped as she saw her father in the midst of them. His laughter stung. He draped an arm behind Prince Alleg while simultaneously shaking Prince Paulsen's hand. Seeing her father, a fleeting pang of regret rolled over her. She tried to imagine what they were agreeing to, and then stopped as her chin started to tremble. Last night had not changed his mind.

Pulling herself together, she hid her doubts behind her formal smile. She concentrated on keeping her chin still, hiding her trepidation. Her steps echoed in the empty ballroom, grabbing their attention. Their conversations stopped, and their eyes darted toward her.

Her father welcomed her with an embrace. "I expect you to behave today," he warned beneath his breath.

She smiled innocently. "That would be my royal duty."

CHAPTER FOUR

The tournament grounds towered on the hillside. Colors streaked through the air. Banners waved, mingling the colors of the visiting royals and their territories with the red of Soron. King Theodore wanted each visitor to feel the power of inclusion in his kingdom.

In preparation for the day's event, stockpiles of weapons, flags, and hay lined the entrances and service gates. The scent of freshly turned dirt mixed with the slight tang of horses in the air. Three distinct sections made up the interior field: an area for archery, the main path for the joust, and the weaponry for the mock battle.

Madeline jumped at the blaring trumpets as they walked through the main gates. The size of the crowd surprised her. Fanfare from trumpets blasted, welcoming the continual swarm of people. In the rush of the crowd, the field came alive with excitement. Just as the ballroom seemed alive with the flowing colors of fire, the fairgrounds bloomed like a spring field. Purples, greens, reds, and yellows filled the stands, every inch a bright spectacle of beauty.

She glided up the pathway to the upper compartments where plush chairs marked their reserved seating. King Theodore marched to his spot and waved to the crowd. The cheers continued to deafen the stadium. Braden sat to the right of his father, smiling and holding Sophia's hand. Madeline saw the empty seat on the left, reserved for her. She smiled at Sophia before taking a seat.

Her heart beat in rhythm with the cheers. Despite her earlier reluctance, she now felt at ease. No one stared at her here.

In the center of the field, the jesters amazed the crowd as they juggled fruits and balls, increasing the numbers of objects until they circled in a blur. The crowd erupted when one of the entertainers picked up a clucking hen. Even her father chuckled.

Madeline loved tournaments. She felt the energy of the people around her, laughing, enjoying the moment. At these events, she disappeared into the crowd, becoming one of the fans. No expectations weighed on her. There were no requirements.

Her gaze strayed toward her father, and she sighed. She knew today would be different. No matter how much she tried to believe he might change, she couldn't ignore the presence of the gawking men. If he chose a champion for her today, her future would be finalized.

She caught her breath when her father stood and cleared his throat. It was beginning.

"Welcome, one and all," the king said. "Thank you for coming on such short notice. Most of the time we try to be prepared, but what is more fun than a spontaneous contest?" He stopped for a second as the crowd laughed.

"This is a momentous occasion. My daughter, our Princess Madeline, is at the age of finding herself a husband." The crowd murmured their appreciation, and she blushed. No longer invisible in the crowd, she felt the heat in her cheeks.

The group of suitors stood together. Prince Paulsen, still dressed in black, winked at her and nodded. His confidence amongst the others was obvious. Prince Alleg blew a kiss before sitting, and Baron Elliot took a swig of his drink. Beside them, at least ten other men smiled at her, crowding in, vying for her attention. She frowned and looked back to her father. His plan seemed broader than she had anticipated.

"With a husband on one side, she needs a knight champion on the other."

Her stomach dropped. The audience roared in agreement and waved their flags back and forth enthusiastically. It seemed the entire crowd agreed with him.

Madeline looked up and saw her father looking at her expectantly. She shook her head, and saw the warning dimple in his smile. All eyes were on her now, and she had to do something. The crowd, the suitors, her father, brother, Sophia, and even the knights on the field watched. Everyone expected something from her.

"Thank you all for coming," she said, her voice cracking as she tried to find the right words to satisfy but not encourage her father. "I'm sure we will be amazed by the feats of these men. I know my life may depend on it." She ended with a small laugh.

It was brief, but enough. As she finished, her father nodded, and the band started up, announcing the main event.

A line of musicians filed onto the field, followed by a troop of jesters carrying various flags. Weaving in and out, they dipped and tossed the flags to the music. After the flags, acrobats tumbled across the field. Jumping off hay bales, over the jousting dividers, and around the poles, they used the field to their advantage. The opening ceremony left her speechless.

One by one, the knights moved into position, playfully chasing the tumblers off the field. Their armor gleamed under the mid-morning sun. In a line, they walked around the arena, waving to the stands, showing off the crests etched into their armor and shields.

As they rounded the final corner, they raised their visors and bowed to the king. Madeline leaned forward in her seat, recognizing the knights from their years of service. She saw Sir Anthony, Sir Reynold, and Sir Marcus, the knights who used to swordplay with Braden. A red sash across each of their shields marked them as knights of Soron. Next to them, several other knights she did not know by name bore the same marking.

The hairs on the back of her neck stood up as the sensation of being watched took hold. She twisted in her seat, almost knocking the red pillow from behind her back. She searched the crowd but didn't see anyone still watching her. All heads faced forward, observing the knights retreat to the sides. Even her suitors had settled back in their seats for the tournament. Looking back to the field, she saw one knight gazing at her, his visor raised up. A red sash covered his shield, but she didn't recognize him. Her cheeks burned, and she glared back defiantly, troubled at the butterflies fluttering in her stomach.

A final trumpet blared, and the events began.

Running onto the field, the knights separated into two teams for the mock battle. Blue tags hung from the sword scabbards of the first team; the other team used red. Each knight was allowed three solid hits before handing over his tag and leaving the game. If his tag was forcefully removed, he was out as well.

Strategically placed around the arena, the teams prepared for battle. When the starting trumpet blared, each flew into action. Swords connected and the clash of metal rang through the air. Each knight worked to their advantage, using speed, agility, and brute strength to defeat their opponent. The hay bales splintered, and blue tags littered the field as the red team dominated.

Centered in the chaos, the trio of her favorite knights worked together, defeating the blue team. Beside them fought the mystery knight. Delivering massive blows to man after man, he ran a circle around the field, finishing with a pile of blue flags in his left hand.

She watched their names move up on the leaderboard. A vertical tower held wooden planks with each knight's name and kingdom. At the far end, the stewards marked tallies to account for points.

She looked to the top and saw the names of her favorites, along with another.

"Sir Daniel," she mused, looking back to the field at the mysterious knight. The name seemed familiar, although she couldn't place him.

After a while, she found it easy to enjoy the tournament. When each new event started, she lost herself in the cheers, the excitement, and the swirling energy.

When the knights paired up for fencing, she admired the fancy footwork beneath their flickering swords. They proved just as handy with the long swords as their broadswords.

Archery, a crowd favorite, surpassed her expectations. In an attempt to outdo their previous tournaments, the knights found new targets to hit. In place of the standard circular targets, smaller items were put up. The crowd erupted as pumpkins and watermelons split beneath the force of the feathered arrows. Winners of the first round competed on apples, pears, and tomatoes.

After each round, she found herself studying Sir Daniel. His fluid movements under the stiff armor and his skill with multiple weapons impressed her. But she was most affected by his simple nod in her direction after each event. She couldn't look away.

In all events, he excelled. Her stomach flipped the higher his name moved up the leaderboard. She couldn't decide if she was more worried about him winning or losing.

The end of the tournament crept closer. Madeline's concentration on the event slowed as the imaginary clock in her mind ticked away.

Something bumped her elbow. Her father beamed at her. "I think we found your knight."

Covering her elbow with her other hand out of reflex, she looked back to the field. The joust was about to begin. The entire stadium stood on their feet, and the trumpets blasted like the end of the world was approaching. More like the end of my freedom, she thought.

The mid-day sun shone down on her, melting her into the seat. No matter how much she fanned her face, small beads of sweat rolled down her temples. The unbearable heat and anxiety twisting her insides wore on her.

The knights lined up for the final event, separating again to opposite sides of the field. Their horses stamped with anticipation as the men grabbed their lances. The joust demanded physical strength, timing, hand and eye coordination, and pure courage. Each contender rode toward his opponent, hoping to unseat the other man. The winner was lucky if he remained on his horse, and the loser felt lucky if he didn't break a bone.

Some of the king's best men fell off their horses in the first pass. She frowned as her favorites lost, and their names were lowered on the leaderboard. Now it was Sir Daniel's turn.

Madeline didn't realize she was holding her breath until her chest burned. Daniel raised his visor in a final salute. As their eyes met, her stomach flipped. He lowered his visor, and she clenched her hands together in anticipation.

Closing her eyes, she heard hooves stomp across the fairgrounds. Each thump matched the beating of her heart. Thump, thump, thump. The smell of the horses, fresh dirt, and dust filled her senses. The cheers grew louder and louder, forcing Madeline to open her eyes.

When she reopened them, she saw Daniel start his approach. His opponent lowered his lance. The event seemed to unfold in slow motion. The rhythm of the hooves, the cheers of the crowd, the waving of the flags... Madeline looked away, suddenly afraid. The men collided like thunder, a chilling sound. She jumped to her feet to see over the heads of the people in front of her. She couldn't see anything, and didn't know what the loud cheers meant.

When she found a hole in the crowd to peek through, she saw the opponent, a knight she did not know, lean back and slide off his horse with a jolt. Daniel leaned forward, holding his chest, but staying up. The crowd exploded. Daniel looked up through the crowd, searching. Lifting his hand to raise his visor, he turned toward Madeline and smiled.

Madeline sat down as a wave of nausea rolled over her. She leaned back in her chair, pale and uneasy. The end of the tournament jolted her back to reality. She didn't need to watch them move the leaderboard; she knew her knight champion had been found.

Her mind spun with the realization. Knowing the next logical step her father would take, she had to make a choice. She looked up just as her father stood and clapped his hands.

***

King Theodore smiled. He couldn't help himself. As he watched Sir Daniel unseat his opponent, his own heart swelled in excitement. No doubt about it, this knight proved himself worthy of guarding his daughter. His velvet robe slipped down his arms as he waved them in excitement.

"Men, women, all my countrymen," he began. "Never before have I seen such determination, strength, and skill. I am honored to have this man as a knight of Soron and protector of our princess. Sir Daniel, it is my privilege to formally introduce you as knight champion of Princess Madeline. May your pledges of loyalty and bravery guide you as you guard my daughter."

Not a single person remained quiet. The whole crowd stood up to cheer the announcement.

King Theodore watched the tournament field with pride. One of his knights proved above reproach his right to the position. The other men surrounded Daniel, clapping him on the back in congratulations. The field began to fill with excited guests and performers. Before the commotion on the field grew, he motioned to his steward on the sidelines of the field.

"With this win, you not only obtain a position of honor, but receive a gift of honor as well."

The steward jumped into action, bringing one of the banners of Soron and a statue of a golden dragon to Daniel. He watched as the knight took the gifts with a look of confusion.

Daniel dropped to the ground and regarded the king. He took off his helmet in salute. Sweat dripped down his face. The king watched his face waver between him and the chair at his side. King Theodore followed his gaze to where Princess Madeline sat.

King Theodore and the crowd gasped as they, too, saw her empty seat.

CHAPTER FIVE

Madeline sobbed. She had held back her tears as she slipped under her seat in the stands, climbing down the wooden posts without uttering a sound, but as soon as she was free from the fairgrounds, she could no longer hold her emotions back.

Her blue gown whipped against her body as her feet flew over the ground, moving as quickly as her heart pounded. The tears flowed freely, blurring the grand façade of the castle in front of her into an obscure mess.

Her soft sobs echoed through the deserted halls as she ran to the safety of her room. Flinging her door open, she threw herself on the bed, hiding her face in one of her pillows. She cried until no more tears remained, leaving red streaks around her eyes and down her cheeks.

"This isn't going according to plan," she muttered, knowing she couldn't avoid the fallout from her actions. The full extent of her disobedience came crashing down on her. In front of her kingdom, she openly defied the king. This wasn't like changing dresses and skipping out on the end of the ball. Her father was embarrassed by that. He would be outraged at this.

She didn't want to think about husbands, or knights, or being a queen. She wanted to feel the wind blow through her hair as she galloped the countryside for fun or watched the sunrise over the Blue Mountains.

"I can't do this anymore!" she yelled, throwing her

pillow against the wall.

In a moment, she had decided. She ran around her room, grabbing the important items and stuffing them into a bag. A couple of her plainest, most practical dresses, her marble brush, leather shoes, a satchel, and a few trinkets to remind her of home. Her head jerked up at the pounding on her door.

"Hold on, I'm coming," she yelled, hiding the bag under her covers. She looked around. The room had disappeared under a mess of thrown dresses and scattered jewelry. Smoothing her dress, she approached the door cautiously, preparing for the wrath of her father.

"Oh, it's only you," she said, her forced smile melting off her face.

Braden walked in behind her and stared at her in disbelief. "You should be glad it's just me. Do you have any idea what you've done?"

"I just left early, that's all," she said, looking at the ground and biting her lower lip.

"You did more than that and you know it. Look at your room," he said, moving a discarded dress with his foot. "You're acting like a little kid about this."

"Braden, you just don't understand. You never have. Our whole life, you've lived up to father's expectations, followed his guidance and rules. I haven't had anyone to guide me. I'm not prepared for these so-called responsibilities. I can't do it."

"What are you talking about? Father has guided you as well."

She looked at her brother sadly. "If you call sending

me to this room whenever something exciting, dangerous, or new is about to happen, then he guided me well."

"Madeline," he said, grabbing her hands. "You're making this a bigger deal than it is. You should be grateful. He's dropping a kingdom in your lap. I'll have to wait at least twenty more years until I will rule here. I've been careful, dutiful, and respectful. Maybe if I displayed half the disobedience you do, I would get more."

She pulled away at his laugh and turned around. He lectured at her, but all she heard was a hum of duty, loyalty, and responsibility. She rolled her eyes and stared at the patterns on the floor. No one was asking her what she wanted. At one more mention of duty, Madeline broke down. Tears trickled down her cheeks.

Braden stopped mid-sentence and dropped to her side. He lifted her chin and looked in her eyes. "I didn't mean to upset you. You know I care about you and want the best for you."

Madeline shook off his hand and tried to stop her quivering chin. "I can't do this," she trembled. "I can't live my life this way, having no choices, no options. That isn't a life." She wiped her tears off her face and slumped back on the bed.

Braden looked at her. "I know. It's tough having our futures laid out for us. But some things are easier when you go along with them. Not everything has to be a battle." He sat down next to her and tossed the scattered pillows behind him. "Did you forget how to clean your room?" he laughed, straightening the bed beside him.

"Braden, no!" she started to say, but it was too late.

"What is this?" he asked, holding her leather bag in one hand.

"Nothing," she said, biting her lower lip and looking down at her toes.

"Nothing?" he demanded.

Madeline's chin trembled beneath his gaze. In moments of anger, he looked like their father. "I'm leaving," she blurted, grabbing the bag from him. "It's the only way."

Braden's gaze darkened. "Leaving? Oh no, you're not." He slammed the door behind him as he ran out the door.

Madeline jumped up, knowing her time was short. He was going to the king.

"It's now or never." She grabbed her bag and ran out the other door on the opposite side of her chamber.

CHAPTER SIX

The sun began to set and hints of pink and orange appeared in the sky. As the tournament ended, people trickled back into the castle leaving the halls mostly deserted. A soft thumping reverberated through the air, announcing the start of an impromptu celebration in the square. That would give her even more seclusion as she skulked through the halls.

The dim light, silence, and cold air settled heavily as she closed the door behind her. Her nose was cold, her feet felt heavy, and she could see her breath when she wasn't holding it.

As she hastened down the halls, she thought back to the tournament. It seemed so distant now. Each step she took away from her room seemed like an extra year added to her life.

Madeline ran down the service routes in the opposite direction of the royal chambers. She didn't have much time for escape, but she knew which halls to take. Years of hide-and-seek and spying games with her brother and Sophia had taught her the secret paths around the castle. She glided through the halls, looking around frantically to make sure no one was watching or following her. Her hair whipped her face with every turn, and her heart pounded in her ears. Luck was on her side; the castle was quieter than usual.

Feeling lightheaded, she let out a deep breath and

rested her hands on the wooden beams of the back door. The cold iron on the handles felt good and solid beneath her fingers. She had never done anything like running away before.

She cursed herself silently for not thinking this far ahead and held her breath as footsteps approached from behind. *Pound, pound, pound.* Either the person was speeding up or her heart was beating way too fast. The sounds were too close to tell.

Madeline pushed the doors open. A rush of cold wind hit her. She made it to the closest tree and sat on the opposite side, feeling the rough bark scratch through her dress. She glanced back at the towering gray castle covered with red banners, waiting for someone to follow. No one did. She turned back and saw the rest of the kingdom stretch out before her. Relief rolled over her.

She saw everything with new eyes. The castle behind her lost its luster, the greens in the fields brightened, and the sky radiated a new beauty. Everything outside seemed so alive to her. Baying dogs, chirping crickets, even the rustling of the leaves were new.

Her breath caught in her chest, tightening her whole body. The silence broke under the rowdy yells of the knights. Leaving the tournament grounds, they passed right by her on their way back to the castle. Though she feared she'd be caught, their warm laughs made her smile.

In the center of the group walked Daniel. She watched him, eager to see more of the man who had worked so hard to become her champion.

He walked at ease with the older men. His helmet and

shield swung from one hand, while the other cradled his prized statue. He was still in his armor, and his face sagged from the long day. As she watched his hair drop over an eye, she fought the urge to move it for him. They wound around the path, disappearing on their way to the castle gates.

One thing was for sure, she thought, closing off her feelings as the men passed. If she stayed behind the tree much longer, she would be found.

Now she just needed to decide where to go. Spinning around, she positioned herself so she faced north. Thinking back to her geography lessons, she thought out her options.

Dragon lairs plagued the northern territories near Dragon's Gate and the southern bay. Everyone said they were long since abandoned, but she decided not to go in those directions. The exiled lands were to the east, and she wasn't ready to consider herself banished forever, so that only left one option. She would go west, through the forest.

She glanced behind her one last time. The castle towers glimmered with their candlelight, vivid banners waving with the wind. For her whole life, she'd been held captive within those stone walls. She tore her eyes away, allowing bittersweet tears to fill her eyes and stream down her cheeks.

"Goodbye." She turned and ran before any more tears could fall.

Skirting behind trees and jumping over rocks, she fled as quickly as possible. She was out of breath by the time she made it to the outlying edge of Soron Village, a world of its own in the shadow of her father's castle. She leaned behind the closest home.

Peeking around the corner, she saw people running. While the castle dozed in the aftermath of the tournament, the village bustled with the rhythms of everyday life. Men returned from working in the fields, lining up their equipment and livestock. Women tidied their gardens and pulled down laundry. The momentary break of the day's event didn't stop life in this community.

She clutched her bag close and felt the smooth silk of her dress. Looking down at her midnight blue gown, she recognized it as a flashing alarm, announcing her identity to everyone. Too late to change. She tried to hide in the shadows of the trees.

She ducked beneath the windowsills, listening to the joy of the families. The air filled with the giggles of children and the lingering scent of ham. Her stomach growled and her mouth watered as the sweet smell hit her. Both hands darted down, trying to stifle the noise, but it didn't work. Afraid that someone might hear, she bent down and ran as low and quick as she could through a wheat field.

The wheat smacked her face, each golden piece striking out at her. Her body flew forward as she tripped over a rock. Throwing her arms out in front of her, she braced her fall, groaning as pain shot through her knees.

Madeline looked back to see what she had tripped over, and stopped. A few feet away, large brown eyes peeked back at her. Their eyes connected for a brief moment in mutual shock. Slowly, she crept closer to the girl, whispering for silence.

The girl, not much younger than herself by the looks of it, glanced back toward the village, fear obvious in her eyes.

"Wait," the princess said, as loud and forceful as a whisper could sound. "I need your help. Please."

The girl looked back at her cautiously.

"I can give you gold," she blurted to keep the girl from scooting away. "All I need is your help and your clothes." The other girl looked down at her apron and then at Madeline's gown. Madeline could see the deliberation in her eyes, shifting from startled fear to hunger and greed.

She looked at the bag of gold in Madeline's hands and untied her stained apron, handing it over to Madeline in a tight package of brown smudges and small rips. It was obviously her work smock and was covered with stains, dirt, grass, and sweat. Madeline scrunched her nose at the smell, but threw it over her head without a second thought.

She looked down and smiled. She no longer looked like a princess. No one would give her a second glance now. She upheld her promise and handed over her gown and the bag of gold. She met the girl's big eyes with her own.

"You've saved my life more than you know. Now, one last thing," she said, leaning in to whisper into the girl's ear.

The girl's eyes widened and she stepped back to

appraise the princess. "Are you sure?"

Madeline nodded. "Thank you."

The girl shook her head and cupped her hands around the bag of gold, making sure none of it spilled out as she ran away.

Madeline's vulnerability faded under her new guise. The commonness of the apron made her feel invisible. Only one more small touch was needed. She bent down and grabbed a handful of dirt, cringing as she rubbed it over her face and through her hair. The grittiness gave her goose bumps. She pulled up the hem of her dress and apron and ran as fast as she could. By the time she reached the forest at the edge of the village, she was out of breath again. With one last quick look around, she closed her eyes and plunged into the woods in front of her.

Sounds came at her: whispers of breezes, birds chirping in the wind, the flapping of wings, and the crunching of twigs. Suddenly the excitement of her recklessness turned to fear. She froze, not so sure about the sounds of freedom.

She moved deeper into the woods, holding her breath, watching the trees thicken around her. A noise startled her. She jumped, trying to force herself to remain still, but nothing happened. Letting her breath out, she convinced herself that she'd imagined it, until she heard it again—a loud branch breaking behind her. Crouching low, with her knees pressed into her chest, she gripped her fingers into the cold dirt. Turning around, she gasped, eyes wide open, as she saw feet racing toward her.

Darkness flooded her vision as the pain came

crashing down on her head.

CHAPTER SEVEN

King Theodore paced his study and slammed his fist on the table. How could she do this to him? He pounded his desk again, toppling over his prized model ship. The delicate masts broke.

A leather-backed chair squeaked as he pulled it away from the table. He hung his head and lifted the small wooden pieces.

"It seems a strong hand can hurt without meaning to," he sighed. The tiny pieces dropped softly. "What am I going to do? A king that can't control his princess. How can I get her to understand?"

His blood boiled the longer he thought about Madeline.

He sighed and looked at the mess on his desk. How had any of it gotten to this point? His eyes filled with tears as they strayed to the portrait of his wife.

"Father!" Braden yelled storming through the door. "It's Made— "

King Theodore's head jerked up at the intrusion. Jumping to his feet, he swung his crimson robe and walked around the desk.

"Young man!" he stammered, "you forget yourself."

"But Father, wait. I have to tell you—"

"What you have to say isn't that important. Nothing is more important than common courtesy," he interrupted, feeling his face redden.

Braden stood quietly by the door.

"Now stand up tall and listen," he ordered. Braden straightened his back.

"Father," Braden tried again, but was silenced by the king's raised palm.

"No, son," he answered sternly, his voice on the verge of cracking. "I will have at least one child that obeys. One day you will be king here, and you'll need to know the importance of patience and timing. You'll need to act according to your station in life. Patience is important, one of the foundations of a respectable ruler. You need the ability to listen and hear both sides of a situation."

He waited, watching his son stand still with a look of obedience on his face. King Theodore smiled. He hadn't lost his touch. The chair creaked as he moved it back to sit down.

"Now," he said, easing himself down. "What is it exactly that made you rush in here, forgetting yourself?"

Prince Braden looked at him, hesitating, making sure it was all right to speak. "It's Madeline, Father," he said. "She's leaving."

"What?" he yelled, pounding his desk. The wooden ship fell over again with a loud crash. "Why didn't you tell me sooner?"

Braden stared back at him, his jaw dropping.

"Of course," the king murmured, "I forbade you. Let's go see if we can talk some sense into her." He walked to the door and slammed it behind them.

With each step he took toward Madeline's room, King Theodore felt his anger rise. When they reached her chamber, he heard silence. He looked pointedly at Braden as he knocked on the door. No one answered.

"Madeline, open the door this instant!" he yelled. Again, no one answered.

He fumed and counted to three, feeling his anger boil with each passing second. His lips tightened, fading to white. Nostrils flaring, teeth flashing, he raised the bottom of his robe and kicked in the door.

The door flew open and banged against the far wall. He stomped around the room, trampling her discarded clothes and dolls.

Braden stood outside the doorframe, peeking in from around the corner.

"Madeline," King Theodore yelled. "Come out now! We need to talk." He walked around the room, looking beneath the covers, behind the plush chair, and in her closet.

"Madeline?" he called out again. Worry strained his voice as he looked down. Lying on the floor in a discarded heap of clothes, the green silk gown called to him. He felt the soft silk drape as he held it in his arms. Tears welled up in the corners of his eyes as he leaned back onto the edge of the pink chair.

Braden shifted back and forth, looking at him with a startled expression. "Father?" he asked, taking a small step into the room.

He didn't even turn around. He couldn't take his eyes off the dress as he spoke to his son. "Braden, go get the men ready. Have them meet me in the grand hall." King Theodore laid the dress out on her bed, smoothing out the wrinkles before walking out. He didn't look back.

The grand hall echoed as he walked to the throne. He held onto the edge of the seat, feeling the cold stone. The silence deepened the pit in his stomach as he waited.

Before long, the knights piled in, running to position before him. When they all appeared, he looked at each in turn. Their red eyes stared at him, questioning their summons. Each face wore a mixed look of exhaustion, excitement, and confusion. In his worry, King Theodore had forgotten about their long day.

He paused as he came upon Sir Daniel, weary from the competition. Beneath his strained eyes, the king saw concern. Daniel knew something was wrong.

King Theodore placed his hand on Daniel's shoulder and nodded. Now was the time for him to prove worthy of his new position. The king needed him to find and protect Madeline, at any cost. He cleared his throat.

"Knights of Soron, brave and loyal men," he said, looking at each in turn. "I ask a lot of you today. This is your moment of truth, your moment to prove your loyalty, and your moment for devotion to our kingdom." He paused, letting his words sink into their tired minds.

"We have lost someone precious, precious to me and to our kingdom. Princess Madeline is missing. I need you to find our princess and bring her back. There is no time to waste. I want you to find her. Find my Madeline," he pleaded.

Questions burned on confused faces. No one knew what to say or where to begin.

"Do not ask. Just go!" he ordered, sinking back onto his throne.

Daniel jumped and gave a final salute before walking out the door. A line of men followed. They were on their way.

"Now to pray they find her quickly," he whispered to himself.

He sat back in his throne. Grief struck him in a way he hadn't felt in sixteen years. A new sense of helplessness rolled over him as the hall emptied.

***

Madeline drifted in and out of consciousness. One moment pain erupted in her forehead, another moment she sank into deep emptiness. Floating in and out, she incorporated her surroundings into her sleep.

She knew her captors were walking. Her body swayed with their footsteps, and pain flooded her head in beat with every step. Pound, pound, pound. There was no relief. Barely opening her eyes, she peeked to see what was happening, but the pain in her head clouded her vision. A musty, sweaty odor lingered in the air and in her nostrils, filling her mind with visions of rotten meat. Trying to concentrate on something else, she felt something sticky rolling down the side of her face. The ropes tying her arms and legs together bit into her skin, deepening the wounds as they moved. She would have screamed, but a rag choked back her words.

She couldn't see her captors, but from their smell and

grunts, she imagined vile-looking creatures. Their muffled voices rumbled, and she started counting the trees that they passed. The trees got thicker and thicker, blocking out all light from above. A pit opened in her stomach and a wave of dread flooded her as she sunk back into darkness. They were going deeper into the forest and there was nothing she could do.

CHAPTER EIGHT

The deep red sun had dipped below the horizon when they began their search. Their trumpets blasted through the night air, announcing the urgency of their actions. At the king's command, the knights spread out to search for the missing princess.

King Theodore separated his men into four groups, each combing a different area. The knights who had served the longest spread north of the kingdom, braving the myths of dragons. Others were deployed to the south, the western forest, and to the surrounding village. No one ventured east toward the exiled lands, a mysterious, abandoned place beyond the Blue Mountains. When people went there, they never came back.

All the weariness from the tournament disappeared under the adrenaline. The castle rang with action. Their armor clanked as they ran over the cobblestones, and their swords jingled as they jumped on their horses. Daniel carefully tied his shield onto the side of his horse as he led a group down to the surrounding village.

On his way to the village, Daniel stole one quick glance to the east. The mountains shimmered in the last rays of the sunset. The reds had faded, almost disappearing into a sheet of twilight blue and gray fog that settled over the horizon. His horse pulled him forward. One last look, and Daniel turned to face the village, hearing the king's words echo in his mind. He intended to prove himself worthy and find her.

For hours, confusion rang through the air. Knights tromped through the village, searching houses and barns. The air filled with the stomping of hooves and cries of the princess's name. Doors opened and closed to no avail. People looked out from their shuttered windows, concerned and curious.

At house after house, Daniel pounded on the door. His desperation grew. No one knew where she was. He had given up hope by the time he approached the last house in the village.

The other knights had finished their search and regrouped near the tournament grounds. He saw their red banners hanging from the sides of their horses. They hadn't found any information either.

He approached the last house on the street and peeked through the windows when no one answered his knocks. A candle flickered in the windowsill, assuring him someone was home.

Cupping his hands against the dusty glass, he saw a family sitting around a table, leaning close in conversation. Out of the corner of his eye, when he turned back to knock again, something grabbed his attention. He took a closer look, and his anger burned.

Daniel didn't stop to knock; he broke down the door.

"Where is she?" he demanded, pointing his sword at the man standing behind the table.

The family looked up, quiet and pale at the intrusion. The father moved forward, knocking the chair behind him. His wife pulled the item off the table and dropped it into her lap.

"What are you doing here?" the man asked. He stood with his arms folded across his chest, a deep scowl on his face.

Daniel faltered for a moment, then stood upright. He was the knight champion. He had every right to be there.

"Princess Madeline," he demanded. "What have you done with her?"

The man paled and glanced back at his family.

"I don't know what you're talking about," he said, moving closer to where Daniel stood. "We don't know where the princess is. Now, please leave."

Daniel stood his ground but lowered his sword. "Sir, I am sorry for intruding, but I saw her gown on the table." He pointed to the man's wife and daughter, who were huddled together, shaking. "I looked through your window, and you were all sitting around Princess Madeline's dress. Now where is she?"

The man's face stiffened.

"Knight, we know nothing about the princess." He pointed to the door and motioned for Daniel to leave.

Daniel refused. Placing his hand back on the hilt of his sword, almost threatening, he pointed again.

"That's her dress. That's the dress she was wearing at the tournament this afternoon. How can you explain that?" Daniel looked at him and then at the family, pleading for help. "I'm not leaving until I get some answers."

The girl looked down at her lap and mumbled something under her breath. Her mother's eyes widened.

"You'd better tell him," the woman said, eyes downcast, as she pulled the dress off her lap onto the table.

The girl looked at Daniel and then lowered her gaze, unable to hide the shame and fear in her eyes. She shifted her glance to her father, then back to Daniel. He almost felt sorry for her, seeing the nervousness in her face. He wondered what type of trouble she would be in.

"We traded. She said she didn't need it anymore, and we traded." She rubbed her hands back and forth. "I know, I shouldn't have, but she begged me." The girl broke down and leaned over to cry in her mother's outstretched arms.

Daniel walked over to her and knelt down, taking ahold of her shaking hands. "Did she tell you anything else? Anything at all?" he pleaded.

She looked him in the eyes. "Yes, she did tell me one thing. She said she was done and was going where no one would find her."

"Did she say where, exactly?"

"She said that the king had exiled her, so that was where she was going." She covered her mouth. "I wouldn't have done it if I knew she was the princess. I never would have let her go." Her words jumbled together in sobs.

Daniel smiled at her before rushing out the door. "Thank you. The king, and especially I, thank you," he said, running from the home as fast as he could. He peeked back in the window. The girl sobbed into her mother's arms, while the father stood behind them, bewildered.

Daniel jumped onto his horse and turned him to the east, not stopping to regroup with the other knights. There was no time to waste.

He rode through the dark of night and the layer of building fog that grew thicker the further he rode. It was as if he were riding over nothing. If not for the occasional rock outcrop, he might have gotten lost.

It wasn't until the fog had lifted that he stopped.

He looked around, feeling the wind blow across his face, and heard an eerie silence. Looking up, he saw the Blue Mountains silhouetted against the morning sky.

***

The king paced back and forth across the throne room, looking up each time someone entered. The sound of his steps echoed through the quiet chamber. It had been hours since the search party began, and all the preliminary reports were negative. No one had seen her, heard from her, or knew anything about where she might be. In a kingdom overflowing with visitors, how could anyone miss her? The pacing didn't help much, but it did keep his mind occupied.

"Father, you're going to wear your legs out," Braden joked as he entered the room.

He shot his son a harsh look, and immediately regretted it.

"Braden, come sit down for a moment." He motioned to the throne. "What do you see?"

Braden rubbed the back of his neck, knowing he had

said the wrong thing. "I see the throne room, stained glass, and our portrait." His words stilled as he looked at the picture of himself and Madeline.

"If I don't pace, son, I see that portrait. And when I look at it, my mind wanders to dark places. There are too many possibilities, too many risks, for me to relax. No son, this isn't one of her games. This is serious."

"I understand," Braden said, nodding.

With one glance at his son, he knew that it was true. "You're going to make a great king someday," he said, giving Braden a sad smile.

"I've been taught by the best."

Their moment broke as someone cleared his throat. At the entrance to the throne room, Prince Paulsen stood, framed by the massive arch doorway. King Theodore heard Braden groan under his breath.

"Prince Paulsen, please come in," he welcomed him.

Prince Paulsen strode toward them, his black boots hardly making a sound. His sword gleamed at his side, and his shirt looked as crisp and smooth as it had at the ball. A crooked smile played at the edge of his lips, growing bigger with each step. His eyes twinkled with delight.

The king felt Braden stiffen beside him.

"Your Majesty," Prince Paulsen said with flourish. "Your Highness," he added with a nod to Braden.

King Theodore smiled in greeting.

Prince Paulsen coughed to clear his throat again. "I was wondering if I might have a word with you, about your daughter."

His heart skipped a beat, and he looked up sharply.

"Madeline? Have you heard any news?" he asked.

"Er…no, Your Majesty, no news yet," Prince Paulsen floundered. He hesitated, looking around at the guards lining the outer edge of the room. "If I might suggest, how would you feel about my men joining the search for your princess?"

"Absolutely! I'm honored to have your men join mine."

"On one condition, of course," Prince Paulsen continued. "Since I am offering my protection, I ask to remain here until their return…"

The king nodded in approval.

"And… when we return her, I thought we could arrange another ball for her return and betrothal," he looked up expectantly as he finished, "to me."

King Theodore rubbed his chin, understanding the implications of the deal. He met eyes with Prince Paulsen and saw his undisguised greed.

"If you bring back my daughter, there's nothing that I could deny you, even her hand."

Prince Paulsen spun around and ran out of the hall. King Theodore heard the uprising of commotion as the prince whistled to his men.

"Father," Braden exclaimed from behind him. "What are you doing?"

"He'll bring her home."

"But, what he's asking for in return. Is that fair?"

He looked at Braden with a tight-lipped smile. "Greed can be a powerful motivator for some. He can bring her back safely, and that's all I want. That's the end of the discussion." King Theodore stood and walked out of the hall.

CHAPTER NINE

The princess woke with a throbbing head. Pound, pound, pound. Each breath she took made it worse. She squinted. Her cheek itched from the dirt that stuck to her dried tears. She shifted, realizing that rough twine bound her arms. Her fingers and toes tingled from the rope's tightness. Everything seemed blanketed in a cloud of gray. Barely any light was coming through to the ground.

Mumbling sounded behind her, and she could smell meat being cooked over a fire to her right. The warmth of the flames didn't reach her, but she heard it crackling and figured she was being kept on the outside of their camp. Close enough if she was needed, but not too close to get in the way.

Madeline winced from the pain in her legs and head. She had never been hit before in her life and was sure she didn't want to be hit ever again.

Closing her eyes, she tried to remain still as she thought up a plan. She'd already escaped a ball full of suitors, a tournament with the whole kingdom watching, and an armed castle with her own personal knight champion. This couldn't be much harder.

The edges of her mouth curled into a smile. When she made it out of here, she'd be free.

Feigning unconsciousness, she overheard snippets of her captors' conversation. For the most part, it was a jumble of grunts, moans, and mumbles, but when they raised their voices, she heard them loud and clear.

"It was her, I tell you. I saw the clothes. It was the same blue she was wearing at the tourney," one man said.

"She never goes beyond the castle walls. Why would she be near the forest?" another asked, not too interested.

"I don't know, but that's her dress," the first man defended himself.

"Is the meat done? Hey, stop that!" another roared. "I just sharpened it."

"Look. We can get her," the first one whined. "Think about it…"

"Mmm…" the second responded, seemingly more interested.

"Think of the ransom or reward. Did you see the diamonds on it? With just one of those we'd be rich."

"Rich don't matter if you can't spend it. The king would have our heads. If we got caught, we'd be dead men," the second man countered.

Laughter roared through the air.

"That old fool couldn't catch me. But if he did, it's just more reward for you." More laughter followed. "I'm going to get her."

"Suit yourself."

Madeline bit her lip harder, hoping she had heard wrong. Her stomach turned just thinking about it. Their laughter did little to calm her. There was no way to warn the girl she had traded dresses with. There was nothing she could do but hope they didn't follow through.

The shuffling she heard in the distance came at her more loudly. She held her breath, forcing herself to remain still, and heard her heart pounding hard in her chest. Each second seemed to last an eternity. The pointed end of a stick bit into her ribs. In agony, she managed to control her emotions and hide the pain. A putrid smell encircled her. With closed eyes, she imagined a large man with a scraggly beard and crooked, rotten teeth poking at her.

"Hey, Mason," he yelled, "How hard did you hit her?" There was more grumbling as he walked away.

Madeline exhaled slowly and relaxed, relieved that they hadn't tried harder to wake her up. She had heard stories about forest bandits. One of her favorite childhood games, knights and bandits, highlighted their thievery and cruelty. Now they didn't seem so innocent.

She needed to think. Here she was, entangled in their ropes and subject to their plan. She needed to get out of here before they forced her awake.

It seemed like forever to her, lying still with her eyes closed. Without something to keep her mind busy, time froze. Even in her room, she always had other activities to pass the time. Thoughts flowed through her mind, but nothing soothed her for long. She sang songs to herself, counted to one hundred, counted in different languages, did anything she could to keep her mind off an itch on her neck that had started to bother her. She knew her only hope was to remain still for as long as possible. Unfortunately, that itch didn't understand and kept getting worse as the time passed.

Madeline shivered. The air chilled around her, her breath clouded, and the ground began to freeze. The crackling of the fire became clearer above the bantering of the bandits, and she crinkled her nose at the obvious smell of stale ale. By the stench, she assumed they'd spilled more than they drank. Laughter and belches rang through the air, growing louder as time passed.

She rethought her plan, knowing the time to act was soon. The plan seemed simple. Simple worked for her. Wait until they were all asleep, untie her legs and arms, and run as fast as she could back toward her home. Once she was back on familiar ground, she could re-evaluate her next move.

The noise got louder and louder as the night went on. The men laughed as they swore, using words she had never even heard before.

She still didn't feel safe enough to open her eyes, so she had to imagine what was going on by the sounds. She cringed every time metal hit metal. She heard trees shake and bushes bend. The noise escalated until there was an eruption of laughter, and then the camp finally fell silent.

After a while, all she could hear was the crackling of the fire, a few snores, and some heavy breathing. Her chance had come. Madeline opened her eyes and looked around. Under the darkness of night, the trees seemed overbearing. Bushes and branches crinkled under a whistling breeze.

In a pile by the fire, their weapons gleamed. The orange flames reflected off sharpened edges and cast horrific shadows. Behind the weapons, she saw the bandits, fast asleep.

Now that it was time and she saw her captors and their weapons, her heart throbbed with fear.

Rubbing her legs together, she loosened the restraints. "Almost, just a little more," she whispered, biting her lower lip as the pain burned through her torn skin. "Just a little more."

She ripped her legs free and began to work on her arms. The knots cut her and no matter how hard she rubbed them together, they refused to give way. She would have to run with her arms bound.

CHAPTER TEN

Daniel stopped. After riding all night, both he and his horse needed rest. The light from the morning sun reflected brilliantly off the snowcapped mountains. Transfixed, Daniel watched in awe. Seven different shades of blue shone over the mountaintops, and a multiplicity of greens popped out from the hillsides.

He found himself at a crossroads. The exiled lands of the east were uncharted. The forest sprawled ahead of him, and the mountain loomed to his left. No clear direction presented itself. He led his horse to a stream, letting him rest beneath the shade of the pines, as he thought. A breeze blew through his fingertips, cooling his sweat-dampened hair.

He was stuck. Nothing marked the path that Princess Madeline had taken: no footprints, no broken sticks, no horse tracks. There were no indications that he was any closer to saving her. Dust scattered dust around him as he kicked the ground.

"If only there was a way to see ahead. Then I could decide," he said to himself. His words registered and he jumped. "Of course! I just need a better vantage point." He ran across the small stream, over scattered rocks, to the base of the mountainside. About fifty feet above him, a small ledge jutted out.

The rocks scraped his forearms and ripped his pants, but he continued climbing. His muscles ached and sweat dripped from his forehead as he pulled himself onto the narrow ledge. The morning light shone on him, stronger above the tree cover. Unfortunately, the new view did not give him any more clues to the princess's whereabouts. Time passed, and the only thing that changed seemed to be the direction the trees swayed.

Daniel felt like screaming. He had made it this far following the lead from the village, but there was nowhere else to go. This was a dead end. There were no signs of her, and, realistically, he doubted she could have made it this far without help or a horse.

"I am her champion!" he yelled into the sea of trees. "Madeline! Where are you! I'm here for you!" Nothing but the wind answered his calls.

After one last gust of wind, he resigned himself to the truth. He wouldn't find her here. Without a trace to follow, he was wasting time. He slid down the steep hill, landing in an unceremonious heap at the base. With legs as bruised as his ego, he prepared to head back to the castle. Maybe they had had better luck.

He hiked back to where he'd tied his horse, and looked around, startled. His horse was gone. He double-checked his spot, noting the streambed lined with hoof prints, the periodic rocks he had jumped, and the full forest in front of him. He kicked the ground in frustration. Now he had lost his horse too. Could matters get any worse?

Invisible eyes weighed on him. His knight training kicked in; his hands strayed to the sword hilt nonchalantly, hiding his readiness. If someone attacked, he would be prepared. To his dismay, nothing happened.

The wind tickled his neck and the rustling trees teased his ears. A sudden wave of lightheadedness rolled over him, knocking him to his knees. Trying to regain his balance, Daniel leaned against the tree, letting go of his sword. Beneath his reach, something warm nuzzled him. Daniel froze. The emptiness around him turned into a crowd. Surrounding him, a group of green-robed men stood, holding the reins to his horse and pointing wands.

Fear filled every inch of his body. He desperately tried to free his sword, but his arm refused to listen to him. He looked closer at their wands and their green robes and recognized them. He knew that he couldn't win. The wizards had found him.

"Please," Daniel begged, "please help me. I need to find the princess."

The wizards convened together, leaving Daniel in silence. He waited as they decided what to do next. A gust of wind blew through the trees around them, and some of the men started to nod, as if they had heard some sort of answer. Daniel sat still on the ground. The men all gathered together, whispering and looking over at him. One of the men stepped forward.

"We will help you," he said, turning to disappear into the thick forest.

A young boy, trying to appear older and useful, grabbed the reins of Daniel's horse. His small hands hid inside the long sleeves of his robe.

Daniel found himself following through the forest. Wizards surrounded him, enclosing him in a circle of green. His fear disappeared into hope. He didn't know exactly what they knew, or what they could do to help, but they seemed willing to try. That was good enough for him.

CHAPTER ELEVEN

Walking into the depths of the Blue Mountains excited Daniel's senses. The hairs on the back of his arms stood up straight and a slight hum filled the air as the trees, rocks, and air seemed to come alive. Slivers of light blinded him as he looked up through the trees. His eyes swept around him with a sense of awe.

The tallest of the robed men raised his arm to halt the group. Daniel's horse gave a little snort at their abrupt stop.

It was odd—he should have been alarmed, but he wasn't. A strange sense of security enveloped him, like he was wrapped in a wool blanket. He closed his eyes, settling into that feeling.

Daniel had no way to determine exactly where in the Blue Mountains they were. The tutors did not teach about the exiled territories. Besides a quick explanation of their treason and banishment, the wizards weren't mentioned.

Judging by the hours they had walked, he figured they were somewhere up in the middle of the mountain. The trees started to thin and large outcroppings of rocks appeared more frequently. When they stopped in front of an oppressive rock wall, Daniel questioned their position. The cliffs of the Blue Mountains stretched hundreds of feet above. Even the most experienced of climbers shrank at their reputation. Out of options, Daniel would do whatever it took.

The robed men left his side and gathered in a circle. Leaning together, their faces disappeared beneath their hoods and created a living wall of green. Daniel's eyes widened as he watched.

For one short moment, the green in their robes shone with absolute brilliance. Daniel rubbed his eyes, but when he looked back, the robes had faded. He brushed the thought away. It was one of the many mysteries of the wizards.

When he looked back at the gray cliffs, his jaw dropped. An opening in the rock wall grew larger by the second.

"Whoa," he said to calm his horse, and himself, holding the reins a bit tighter.

The wizards ushered Daniel forward. He felt their wands press into his back when he stopped mid-step. A sparkling cave of wonder stood before him, not at all like the empty, damp cavern he had expected.

"Don't let appearances fool you," the youngest wizard whispered, running past him.

Daniel couldn't help but stare. The sides of the cave glimmered in trailing waterfalls. Small pools gathered at the base of the walls, collecting the water into a reflection of light and color. The further he walked inside, the more awestruck he grew.

Ornately carved homes lined what appeared to be the back of the cave, and trails of moss and broken cobblestones marked a path below him. He continued to walk in silence, looking about him. The intricate stonework revealed speckles of pinks, purples, and blues. He couldn't speak; his eyes and mind were transfixed by its beauty.

"Who are you?" he finally asked, finding his voice.

"I'm surprised you have to ask." The tall man smiled and pulled back his hood to reveal his face. A foot taller than the other men, the wizard offered a gentle smile. Carrying himself with the confidence of experience, his look was kind, but also demanded respect.

"You're the wizards of Soron," Daniel said timidly, looking behind at the growing bevy of people peeking around the man who spoke. He was surprised at the large number of women and children among them.

"I am Elias, leader of the exiled." Elias looked more closely at him and winked. "You may have heard about us." He continued walking deeper into the cave.

"We're really not all that different from you and your villagers in Soron, despite what you may have heard. We enjoy a simple life." Elias waved a stable boy over to take his horse.

"How did you know I am from Soron?" he asked, blushing as Elias nodded to his shield and the sash hanging from his horse.

"The real question is not where you are from, but who you are." Elias said.

"I'm Sir Daniel, knight champion for the Princess Madeline," he stammered.

"No, that's your name and station. Who are you?" Elias looked expectantly at him, as if he could see more than what his words conveyed.

"I don't understand," Daniel replied.

"Honest and humble. That's interesting in a knight of

Soron."

"Look, I don't have time for games. I am looking for Princess Madeline. She's gone missing. Have you seen her?"

A soft murmur breezed through the surrounding group. He turned to see the men and women whispering together with looks of excitement and confusion.

Elias shot his hand up and gave the crowd a warning look before turning to face Daniel. The buzz quieted as the tall man looked at him seriously. "I'm sorry. The truth you seek isn't here."

Daniel looked beyond Elias to the rest of the wizards. Their shadowed faces showed they knew more than they were allowed to say.

"What aren't you telling me?" he demanded. "You said you would help. If not, I need to return to my kingdom."

He turned and stormed in the direction of the cave entrance, feeling the weight of their gaze on his back.

"You are right. Please return, Sir Daniel. We may not be able to help you directly, but we can lead you to something that can. The mirror sees all: near, far, here, there, now, and ever. You may find the answers you seek within its images."

Elias waved him back. "Before you go, please rest here, and in the morning we will guide you to the mirror."

"I don't need sleep. I need to find the princess. If you can help me, do it now," Daniel pleaded.

Their gazes met in a silent battle of wills. In an instant, a familiar wave of lightheadedness rushed over him.

"You must understand, good things come to those who wait. In this case, rest will help. Please follow me." Elias held out his hand.

The desire to fight fell away. Hesitant but resigned, he followed the wizard back into the depths of the cave. The crowd fell away, silently watching as he passed. He felt their gazes as they passed the first row of houses.

The old wizard led him to a small home with a thatched roof. Spiral carvings marked the doorway and window boxes. Instead of flowers, trailing ivy overflowed from the window to the ground. Elias held open the door. Daniel shuffled in, finding a single bed against the back wall and a desk positioned beneath the window.

"Now sleep, Sir Daniel, and we'll see what revelations your dreams may bring."

His eyes fell under the full weight of the wizard's command. Through the smallest slivers of sight, he watched the door close and darkness take over.

Dreams hit him in full force, with vivid realism.

Daniel felt the wind blow against him as he rode his horse. The powerful steed that led him to the Blue Mountains carried him far and fast. His chest burst with excitement. He didn't know his mission, but he knew he was riding for his life. The sun set in the distance, a meld of bright, vibrant greens that put the sunsets of Soron to shame.

With a quick move, the sun closed and re-opened, winking at him, teasing him to catch up. He kicked his horse to go faster, chasing the setting sun. As the bright golden ball set beneath the horizon, the scene changed.

He stood back in the armory; soft hammering and the scraping of polish sounded in the background. It was a comforting noise that balanced the hard work of setting and fixing steel. The smooth silver armor twinkled as he polished the edges. He saw his own reflection staring back, and, behind him, bright green eyes watched from the shadows. He turned to search the darkness but saw no one. The blackness of the shadows covered him, and the scene changed again.

On his horse again, the sun shone on him, warming his back under his thick robe. The chase burned in him. He didn't know what he was pursuing but felt its importance. An overwhelming desire to catch it raged in his heart. He kicked his horse harder, trying to get closer. A green light surrounded him until everything shone with a green hue. In an instant, the light burst into thousands of pieces, flying off in different directions. Green butterflies danced in the wind. He fell off his horse trying to catch the scattered green beauties.

Morning came slowly for Daniel. Soft light filtered in through the window as a harmonic chant grew in the background. Then, all at once, he remembered. Not wasting a moment, he slicked his hair back and jumped out of bed. He opened the door, and his jaw dropped, unprepared for what met him.

Standing in front of him, the villagers had lined up, winding a path to the center of the cave. His steps slowed as he passed each person. Their strange smiles unnerved him.

Once he began moving, he couldn't stop. Each person's unwavering smile encouraged him, melting his hesitation. He followed the path of people around the village to the main fountain where Elias stood.

The elder wizard looked pensively into the water.

He cleared his throat. Elias turned with a smile, causing a small ripple in the fountain.

"I trust you rested well," Elias greeted him.

Daniel looked down before answering, feeling the weight of the wizard's gaze. "Not the most restful," he stammered, "but full of interesting dreams." Daniel jerked his head to the wizard, feeling an urge to continue. "Elias, I need your help. Please don't force me. I've been honest to this point, but I don't like being coerced to talk."

A gasp ran through the crowd behind him.

Elias looked at him thoughtfully and smiled, motioning for the crowd to relax. "You are right. It's not often we have guests, and I have forgotten my manners. I imagine our years of exile have put us on edge as well. I'm sorry. Please continue, if you will. I wish to hear about your dreams."

Embarrassed, but appeased, he continued. "There were three sets of dreams. In all of them, bright eyes followed me, just out of reach. I never got to them. I'm not sure what it means. Do you know?"

"Oh yes," Elias said, as if that had brought something to his mind. He turned back to the fountain. They stood in silence for a few minutes, listening to the water flow—a soft, caressing noise. Elias sat on the fountain's edge, as if in deep thought. "And perhaps it will mean more to you in time. I will tell you how to get to the mirror now."

"I thought you were going to guide me," he said, surprised.

"I will guide in the only manner we can. The journey to the mirror is a personal experience; any more and the vision will be skewed. This is your journey—your truth. It is visible only to you. Life is made up of a string of events and choices. What you see is yours if you choose it to be." He stopped and raised his eyebrows at Daniel.

Daniel nodded to show he understood.

"These choices can create harmony and peace, but they can also destroy," the wizard finished, handing him an old folded map. "The mirror will find you when you are ready to see." Elias grasped Daniel's forearm and looked him in the eyes. "Farewell, Daniel, I hope we meet again. And I hope you find what you seek."

They walked to the entrance in silence. He numbly took his horse's reins and walked out the entrance. When he looked over his shoulder to say goodbye, the door had already closed.

CHAPTER TWELVE

Madeline slipped her left foot from the ropes that tied her legs together, grateful to be free of its biting grip. A tingling sensation ran through her legs as the blood returned. After lying still for so long, her body resisted each movement. She breathed deeply and looked around, remaining as silent as she could. Her eyes scanned the camp as she got her bearings.

All the men appeared to be asleep. She took a quick count: one, two, three, four, five—only five men. With the amount of noise they had made, she had imagined more than that. It both surprised and calmed her.

Madeline tiptoed through the scattered leaves, strewn clothes, and discarded weapons as she approached the fire. Its warmth put her at ease. Despite her circumstances, she found herself studying her captors. Knocked out, either by the fighting or the ale, they appeared quite harmless.

She had pictured grotesque monsters, but these men appeared quite normal, though big, burly, and covered in hair and dirt. She wrinkled her nose against the offensive smells rising from each as she bent closer.

One of the men, closest to the fire, didn't look at all like she had pictured. Small and skinny, with scars etched in his hands, he looked prematurely old. His smooth cheeks showed him to be closer to her age, perhaps only a few years older. A wave of pity hit her as she looked at him and thought about the life he had chosen. A life of freedom did not have to mean a life of thievery.

As she turned to walk away, her eyes stopped on the orange flames. Glittering behind the fire, something sparkled like jewels. A pang of regret hit her as she remembered that she'd given her only bag of gold to the peasant girl in return for the work smock. In her haste, she'd overpaid; a few pieces would have been sufficient. Now, as she contemplated the sparkle, she realized what that money could buy—all the pieces of her plan she hadn't prepared for. It would mean safe passage through the forest, food, shelter, new clothes, and possibly a new life.

She walked around the fire, cringing as the branches broke. Even with cautious steps, her movements announced her escape. As she glanced between the sleeping men and the treasure, her heart beat wildly.

She leaned over to grab the gold, and her heart dropped. It wasn't gold. Instead, a small dagger gleamed, its golden hilt reflecting brilliantly in the firelight. Not her first choice, but still useful. She grabbed at it. The weighted handle felt awkward in her hand. She had handled knitting needles, instruments, and books, but never a weapon. As strange as it felt, it gave her a sense of relief.

She clutched the knife as someone spoke. Low words, jumbled together. She froze, waiting for a new blow to her head, but nothing came. Braving a glance behind her, she sighed with relief. It was time to go.

Lifting the hem of her apron, aware of the hidden branches, she crept away from camp. The crackling of the fire faded as she moved away. She counted again and saw the sleeping men. One, two, three, four—one was missing. Her hair swept in front of her eyes as she spun around.

She had waited too long. No longer fearing the crunch of breaking branches, she ran. Her heartbeat echoed as she whipped around, looking behind to make sure the path stayed clear. Branches struck her, scratching her arms and face as she slipped deeper into the thick forest. She followed a narrow trail as it wove between the bushes and trees.

After a few moments, her relief changed to dread. Stepping around a tree into her path, the fifth man appeared, cutting off her route. His dark, menacing eyes glared at her.

She scrambled back, stumbling over her own feet, feeling the rough ground underneath her palms as she fell. Whimpering, she edged her way backwards, stopping against the rough bark of a tree. It was the youngest of the bandits. Her sympathetic feelings for him disappeared as she saw the hard, hungry look in his eyes.

"Where do you think you're going?" he asked, grinning.

"Stop," she whispered, and then, louder, "Stop!"

"Who's going to make me?" He laughed, walking toward her. "You?"

Madeline kicked her legs, spraying dirt and leaves behind her as she ran around the tree.

"Come back!" was all she heard. She scrambled back through the forest and broke into a run. The trees around her all seemed the same. With no sense of direction, she bolted, hoping her path would lead her home.

As she fled, the air came harder and harder into her chest. The cold created a thick fog in front of her. A cramp rose in her side. This was not what she had planned. Her thoughts raced, distracting her from the roots bulging up from the ground.

She brought her hands up just in time to break her fall. Struggling, she made it back onto her hands and knees but heard laughter from behind. His chuckle filled her ears, and tears spilled out of her eyes.

"No," she pleaded, dragging her body forward along the ground as she saw him walking up behind her. "No," she repeated through her tears.

"Oh yes," he said as he grabbed her leg. "Oh yes," he repeated, lifting his arm to hit her.

Pain seared through her. She had only a few moments before the darkness came flooding over her again. The dagger, she thought, remembering her new weapon. The blade bit into her skin as she pressed it between her palms. She prayed that it would stay hidden as she sank back into darkness.

CHAPTER THIRTEEN

Daniel hurled the map down in frustration. Throwing up his arms, he kicked the dirt around him. He had followed the directions step by step, but there was no sign of the mirror. After traveling all morning, it pained him to be at another dead end. First he couldn't find the princess, and now he couldn't find a simple mirror.

His horse looked at him and whined his own frustrations.

"All right, all right," Daniel muttered under his breath, picking up the map. His horse pulled the reins frees and walked off toward a small grassy patch. Leaning against a tree, Daniel shook the dust off the papers.

"This has to be it," he said to himself.

Daniel looked down at the map and then around him. He saw the mountains to the north, the deep forests behind him, and the lake in front of him. Everything lined up with the images on the map, just as Elias had said. This had to be the place.

The area he had been sent to was beautiful. Surrounded by towering pines, a secluded lake backed up to the cliffs. The gray stone walls reflected off the surface of the water. Bright stones lined the crescent-shaped shore. After enduring centuries of soft movement, the rocks were polished smooth. A grove of pines stood a few hundred feet back. Only the soft gurgling of the water upon the shore could be heard.

Despite his peaceful surroundings, he grew anxious. The mirror could be anywhere.

Daniel started his search on the shoreline. Taking off his boots, he felt the soft stones beneath his tired feet. The rounded rocks and cool sand felt good. He studied each foot of land, noticing strange etchings on the driftwood. Water rushed up over the sand, smoothing out the shoreline. Under the gentle waves, Daniel saw something sparkle beneath a large chunk of wood.

The object was shiny and reflected the light, but it was just a polished shell about the size of his palm. He flipped it over, amazed at how the sun bounced off its surface and reflected in a rainbow of color. Smiling, he slipped it into his pocket.

Daniel continued walking along the shoreline until he reached the eastern edge. The trees continued to the base of the rocky cliffs. He found nothing. He had searched every inch of the shoreline, and there was nothing.

"Could the wizards have led me astray?" he murmured. The wizards were known for their acts of treason. They had even used their persuasion on him. Friends or foes, they were too formidable a force to ignore.

"No," he shook his head, clearing his mind. "Elias promised he'd lead me to her. He wouldn't lie about that. I'm just not finding it." He sat on the edge of the shore, feeling the water lap over his toes. "What exactly did he tell me? 'When you are ready, the mirror will show you your way.'"

He stood and brushed himself off. "I am ready to

see," he yelled into the woods. "Show me the way." When nothing happened, he fell to his knees, grimacing as the small pebbles poked into him. "Please," he whispered in desperation.

A fish jumped in the middle of the lake. Daniel watched the images of the fish reflect off the lake's surface as it jumped, creating a perfect double image.

Of course.

He leaned forward to see his reflection. How could he have missed it? The lake itself was the mirror. He had spent the entire day looking for something that was staring right back at him. Shaking his head, he laughed.

"Show me the princess," he said, watching as the lake filled with colors.

Reds, oranges, yellows—the sunsets of Soron. Daniel was silent, captivated by the transformations in front of him.

The reflections shifted into images and moving scenes. The collage solidified, showing a clear image of the princess.

Daniel jumped. "Princess Madeline, can you hear me? Are you all right?"

The image of the young woman did not answer. Sitting with her back to him, rope bound her arms. Around her, shadows of trees and men towered over her. Before he could shout out again, the scene faded.

"Wait! I wasn't ready! I need to see her again."

The lake answered his request with a new vision. More colors. Her midnight blue gown stained with pools of dark blood. Daniel cried out, unwilling to believe this image. "That can't be all!" he shouted. "I've traveled all this way to find my princess! There has to be more! Help me find her first!"

A new vision appeared, blurred by the stinging tears in his eyes. He saw an older version of himself. Deep lines etched his face as he gazed off into the sunset. The picture expanded, and he saw that on one side of him stood a dragon and on the other, a castle. As quickly as it had appeared, it changed, showing a final image.

The sun had almost set, and the lake filled with red. The vision seemed distorted. Daniel leaned in for a better view and jumped as eyes appeared. The same green eyes that had haunted his dreams in the wizard's cave now fluttered at him in the lake. Their burning intensity captured Daniel's heart so that he didn't notice how far he was leaning forward.

A familiar persuasive feeling wrapped around him, bringing him closer to the water. He needed those eyes. Caught up in the moment of anticipation, he didn't notice the lake coming closer to his face. He closed his eyes, anticipating the touch of her lips, and yelled with surprise when he fell into the cold water.

Daniel gasped for breath. The lake chilled him to the bone. He looked back toward the shore and saw his horse staring at him.

"I know, I know," he mumbled to himself as he stepped out of the lake. He didn't feel his body shivering or the heavy weight of his wet clothes. He could think only of those green eyes.

CHAPTER FOURTEEN

Everything seemed fuzzy to Madeline. She knew the last few days were real; her bruises and bumps proved it. But she wished they were a nightmare. Her head pounded as she woke up, a reminder of her failed escape. She had underestimated these men as simple bandits, but now she knew better. Behind their crudeness lay cruelty to match.

She strained her eyes, but her vision blurred to gray. In addition to the ropes that bound her wrists and legs, a fabric rag covered her head and mouth. The scratchy cloth stuck to her cheek and reminded her of stale bread. Compared to the stench of the men, this was bearable.

It seemed to her that they had brought her back to camp. She heard the familiar crackling of the fire and the deep rumbling of their voices. Everything seemed the same, except for the addition of a new cry. Barely audible, she heard a girl's voice crying out, intermixed with their deep voices.

"Ouch, what're ya hitting me for?" one of the men yelled.

"You idiot, that's not the princess!" Madeline recognized the voice of the scrawny man.

"What do you mean it's not her?" a new voice piped in. "That's the same dress."

"Use your eyes, men. The dress may be the same, but this is not the princess."

A moment of silence stretched between them. The

girl's muffled screams wailed in the background. Madeline's salty tears soaked into the rag binding her mouth, but she didn't dare utter a word.

"The princess does not have golden hair," the smaller man said.

Grunts of understanding sounded from the other men.

"You idiot, what have you gotten us into?"

"Ouch, stop hitting me."

"I will when you come up with a plan. I won't have two sniveling girls in this camp, you're bad enough."

She held her breath at their silence.

"Look, even if she's not the princess, it's a royal dress. The golden trim is worth something and these diamonds up top are worth a fortune," one said.

"You're right," the smaller man agreed. "The dress may be worth it but not the girl. She'll bring us no ransom. Get rid of her. And be careful. I don't want to see any more stains on the dress, not if we want to get any money for it" he ordered.

"Get rid of her?" he choked.

"Yes. I don't care how. Just make that crying stop."

"Yes sir," he grumbled. "What about the other?"

She inhaled, her heart thumping in the silence before the bandit responded.

"She's mine to deal with," he chuckled.

As their grumbles silenced into sleep, a deep pit opened in her stomach. Madeline exhaled and bit her lip. She needed a plan, quick.

She rubbed her head back against the tree, feeling the

tender spot where they had hit her, above her right ear. Gritting her teeth, she scraped the tied rag against the bark until it loosened. Through the small gap, she saw dim, gray patches of light. In the early morning light, it would be harder to escape. She needed to go now.

Without warning, a loud smack followed by a scream echoed in the woods.

"Now go, before I change my mind!" a man yelled.

The girl's sobs faded into a faint rustling in the woods, and then silence. She was gone. Madeline hoped the girl could find her way back home. Home. It seemed so far away.

A sob stuck in her throat.

Keeping quiet, she rubbed at her restraints until her skin burned under the rope. She felt the light touch of the morning sun. Time was running out if she hoped to escape before enduring another day of capture.

The silence did not last long. Less than an hour later, before the sun fully warmed camp, rumbling grew. The heavy breathing of horses and stomping of hooves burst into the camp. She pressed her body against the tree, hoping to remain unnoticed.

She jumped at a commanding voice.

"Have you seen the princess?"

"The princess," one of the bandits snickered. "I'm afraid we haven't been honored with her presence here in our humble camp."

"Do not joke with matters of royalty," the stoic voice replied.

"I do not know what you mean, good knight. We are

simple men of the forest."

"Simple men with this?" a new, deeper voice asked.

"Seize them at once," the knight boomed, drawing his sword.

"Wait, I can explain," the smaller bandit cried.

"Explain these bloody stains then."

A manic chuckle spread through camp. "She wouldn't be quiet. We had to teach her our ways."

"And we'll teach you ours," the knight responded.

A dozen swords were brandished.

Madeline didn't want to be there if things got worse.

The fighting escalated. Behind her, screams rang out, muffled under the heavy stomps of horses. Metal struck metal, and the familiar grumbles turned to grunts and outcries.

"Give us the princess!"

Her heart leapt as she struggled to free her hands and mouth.

The small, wiry man laughed. "Your princess is gone. There's nothing of her here."

"Then prepare to die!" a strong voice boomed.

"No," she yelled, wishing they could hear her. "I'm here!" she cried, her voice no louder than a whisper.

Screams ripped through the air and swords clashed on shields. The dirt moved with the pounding hooves as men trampled through camp, turning over bushes and knocking down branches from above. The screams of pain were worse than anything she had ever heard. A deep thud sounded next to her, and before she could turn away, she found herself face to face with the small man. His eyes were sightless, empty.

Fear pumped through her, and with a scream, she fumbled forward on her hands and knees. She jumped past the closest grouping of trees and fell backwards over the top of a hill. A blur of green, brown, and blue mixed before her eyes as she toppled over the edge and rolled down the steep side.

She spun out of control, feeling the wind blow against her and small rocks bite into her ribs and legs. Between the moments of fear and terror, brief flickers of excitement hit her.

The pain grew with each jab of a new rock or twig hitting her. The tumble gave way to an abrupt stop as she slammed against a large boulder. Pain shot through her body, and for a moment she lay still. The restraints around her mouth had loosened in the fall, and for the first time since she had left the castle, she felt a smile fill her face.

"Ouch," she yelped as something sharp cut her hands. A stream of blood ran between her palms. Through the chaos of being recaptured, knocked out, and dragged back to camp, she had forgotten that she had palmed the stolen knife. For once, she welcomed the pain.

The cool hilt of the dagger weighed down her hands. Twisting it between her fingers, she found a way to comfortably rub it against her legs and wrists to break the ropes. It took longer than she expected, but when the ropes snapped, so did her composure.

Madeline sighed with pleasure—it felt so good to have her hands unbound—and leaned back against the rock, letting tears well up. She had never felt so happy to be alive. She leaned her head back and listened to the birds between her sobs, hearing the sweet sounds of freedom and rubbing the tender bruises on her ribs.

She was free.

CHAPTER FIFTEEN

The morning sun rose over the castle. Nights seemed to lengthen under the extended search for Princess Madeline. Patrols ran every hour of the day. Guards lined the castle morning and night, stewards questioned the villagers for any news, and scouts were sent ahead to all the territories. He did not spare one home, village, or kingdom in his search. As long as she remained missing, he remained awake and the kingdom on alert.

Golden hues shone through the stained glass windows above his throne. His soft boots scuffed on the floor as he paced a trail around the empty hall. Morning hours tended to be quiet, but every day, fewer visitors appeared. Except for his trusted stewards and guards, no one approached him. The normally cheerful room had darkened.

He continued pacing behind the throne, numbly watching the guards change shifts. Their bloodshot eyes and uncharacteristic slouches spoke of their exhaustion. Maybe he had pushed them too far. They needed rest. He wondered when he'd lost touch with what other people needed.

Leaning against the throne, he felt the cool stone and sighed.

"Is there any news from outside?" he asked as the new stewards filtered in.

"No, Your Majesty. No news as of this morning.

They will find her. I know they will." The steward stood straight against the wall, looking refreshed and polished for service.

"I hope you are right," he said, scratching his chin. Its scraggly surface surprised him. In the days he'd been waiting for news, he had neglected to take care of himself. He felt the rough and sagging skin around his eyes and could see the wrinkled edges on his robe. Every moment spent waiting just added to his weariness.

"Maybe it's time I get some rest as well," he said.

His men nodded but did not respond.

The door to the throne room crashed against the wall. All heads jerked to the back of the room. Striding toward him, a group of men approached, led by a man cloaked in black.

"Your Majesty!" Prince Paulsen called, running into the room. The normal polish that surrounded the prince had disappeared under a layer of dirt. The charming smile people knew him for was noticeably absent from his face.

"Prince Paulsen," the king returned the greeting, jumping down to meet him.

"Your Majesty," the prince began, kneeling. Covering his heart with one hand, he looked at the ground, refusing to meet the king's eyes. "I am deeply troubled to bring you this news."

"Tell me. Have your men found anything at all? Remember, if you bring her back home, she'll be yours." He stopped talking when he saw the prince's men hesitate in the doorway. Their armor was stained with blood, and their heads hung low.

"What happened, Prince Paulsen?" he asked, hiding his shaking hands beneath the thick sleeves of his robe.

Prince Paulsen waved his men forward. They approached slowly, keeping their eyes on the floor. The man in the back looked the most uncomfortable.

He vaguely heard the words but did not move his eyes from the dress draped in the man's arms.

"King Theodore," Prince Paulsen began, his words thick with emotion. "I wish I came with different news, but we were too late."

The throne room seemed to spin. "Did you find the men who did this?" the king asked, in a voice no louder than a whisper.

"Yes, we did. We came upon their camp this morning, in the darker regions of the forest. When we asked if they had seen her, we discovered the truth. I am so sorry. I vowed to bring her home, but not like this."

The king didn't respond. He couldn't say anything. His eyes focused on the blue dress that hung lifeless in their arms.

The prince continued.

"We rode deep into the forest through the night, tracking any signs we could find. There weren't many. We talked to anyone we could—hunters, forest men. A few mentioned a group of bandits that had been terrorizing the area. So we went in search of them. It was early this morning when we finally found them. We surrounded them from every angle," Prince Paulsen stopped for a moment to keep his emotions under control. "One of my men saw this. When we noticed the gown and listened to their mocking words, we were outraged. The fight was brief and complete."

Prince Paulsen's voice shook as he finished the story and rejoined his men.

The room around the king fell silent, and his vision blurred. He was the king of a kingdom, but utterly alone. "I don't understand. How did we go from one disagreement to this?"

"Your Majesty, I vow to turn this tragedy into something grand, in memory of the princess. I will clear that forest of all bandits. No more harm will come to your kingdom." After a quick bow, Prince Paulsen waved to his men to follow and stormed back out the door.

The room returned to silence. The stewards and knights regrouped in their positions. Everyone watched, but no one spoke. No words could adequately fill the void.

King Theodore dropped to his knees and tentatively reached toward the dress. The midnight-blue gown looked dull in his hands. Any luster it held faded without her in it. He smelled it, hoping for a lingering scent.

"Madeline!" he sobbed into the fabric. "Madeline!"

His anguish echoed throughout the hall.

CHAPTER SIXTEEN

Daniel woke up shivering. His feet froze, and his clothes clung to him. A night's sleep hadn't helped him dry off or forget falling into the lake. Rubbing his eyes, he dragged the gritty dirt over himself with his sleeves.

Sitting up, he hunched closer to the fire. As he warmed his hands, his mind drifted back to the lake's images and the magic that haunted his dreams. Lost in thought, he didn't see the wizards until they surrounded him. He tried to speak, but Elias silenced him with a look.

The wizards stood stiff behind Elias, hiding their emotions in rigidity.

Elias squinted through the trees to the morning sun as he spoke. "I trust you found what you are looking for?"

Daniel nodded.

"I hope you understand that you have seen something special, something only a handful of people within or outside the wizarding community are privy to. We expect you to honor that secrecy. But now, Sir Daniel, knight of Soron, you must leave. Take the knowledge you have gained and make your choices."

One of the younger wizards handed him the reins to his horse. He continued to stare at the wizards, dumbfounded.

Elias shook his head. "I am sorry to rush you, but the king needs you. We have spoken with your horse, and he will carry you back as fast as he can. You must hurry."

Daniel didn't understand. He was still tired, and his head ached from sleeping on the hard ground. "I don't—" he started.

"Go," Elias said, his robe glistening in the morning sun. "Go," he repeated as he disappeared back into the forest. The rest of the gathered men stood still, waiting for Daniel to move.

He let out a deep breath and gathered his bag. He knew better than to argue with a wizard. Even his horse neighed impatiently.

"I'm coming, I'm coming," he mumbled.

Turning to thank the men, he watched as they methodically erased all evidence of his presence. One smoothed the soft dirt, another scattered the charcoaled wood, and a last leaned over the lake's edge.

Daniel secretly wished the man would fall in.

"Good day, wizards. Meeting you was an experience I shall never forget." And with a strong kick, he and his horse were off, riding back to Soron.

He rode hard all day, surprised at their fast pace. Even buoyed with the magic of the wizards, there was a lot of distance to cover.

The news of Princess Madeline reached him before he was even halfway there. Men from the outlying territories told him about the king's grief and Prince Paulsen's story. The whole kingdom mourned for its princess.

"The mirror was right," he swore, kicking his heels into his horse. Anger burned within him. He needed to see the king.

The mountains disappeared behind him as he raced across the flatlands. The monotonous landscape blended together in his unsettled thoughts. All at once, he looked up, amazed. On the horizon, the broad castle stood, its banners waving. He was almost home.

The horse stomped through the surrounding village, past the thatched homes and tournament grounds, until it stopped beneath the imposing castle gates.

Throwing his reins to the young boy standing at the gates, he raced toward the throne room. His boots barely made a sound as he flew through the courtyard. The display cart for the bakery tipped over, knocking loaves of bread and fresh apples to the ground. Men and women jumped out of his way as he pressed through the crowd. He didn't stop to explain himself or apologize for the smashed goods. The only apology he had was for the king, for not finding the princess in time.

A gasp rang out around him as he dashed into the throne room. No one moved when he approached the king. He slowed and looked around. Sheets shrouded the stained glass windows, hiding the chamber in shadows. The red banners had been lowered, and the portraits on the back wall were covered. Everyone stood to the side, eyes downcast, mouths closed. No one uttered a word or moved, afraid of disturbing the sanctity of the king's grief.

King Theodore sat on the throne with a wrinkled robe and bloodshot eyes. The midnight blue gown dangled over his legs, and fresh tears rolled down his cheeks.

Daniel approached the throne slowly and knelt before the king. "King Theodore, I have failed you. I could not protect our princess. I am sorry." He waited for a response, but none was given. The king buried his face back in the dress and wept.

Daniel stood back up, feeling the sting of the silent rejection, and retreated to the door. He didn't know what he'd expected, but he understood the king's reaction. For the first moment since hearing the news, he felt it in his heart. The princess that he loved was gone.

Excusing himself from the throne room, he wandered through the gardens. He found himself remembering the brief moments they had shared together. He sat on the marble bench in the rose garden and took a deep breath. His fingertips brushed against the smooth, cold marble, and he smelled the fresh scent of roses, Madeline's favorite flower. Memories of his knighting ceremony and the single white rose made him smile.

He remembered the tournament, watching her as he lined up, memorizing her image and grace. The crowds had noticed him too, cheering his every win and reveling in his challenges.

Most important, he remembered her eyes, those bright green eyes of hers that stared back at him, challenging him, leading him, haunting him in his dreams.

He sat there, full of longing and a strange feeling that he was missing something. Something big.

A moment of clarity hit him. The dress! Princess Madeline hadn't been wearing the dress. She had worn it to the tournament but traded with the village girl. She wasn't the one wearing the dress!

Daniel jumped up, hope filling his heart. "She's

alive!" Daniel said to himself. "She's alive! There's still a chance."

He bolted from the courtyard.

The young boy at the gates handed him back the reins. Other knights called to him, but he didn't stop. He couldn't stop. He was going to save his love. He kicked his feet hard, urging the horse forward as the gates slammed shut behind him.

Before long, he found himself at the edge of the forest. Something stirred inside him, and he knew he was where he needed to be. He weaved in and out of trees, kicking his horse to go faster and faster, feeling the branches whip across his face, stinging his skin. It didn't matter. Nothing mattered anymore except for finding Madeline.

CHAPTER SEVENTEEN

Madeline smiled. The sun warmed her face and hands, the birds sang hello, and a soft breeze whispered congratulations to her. She had made it. She was free. Madeline opened her eyes and looked around to get her bearings. She could see the hill she had rolled down. It was steep and covered with rocks of varying sizes. She ran her fingers over her ribs and winced; they were still sore. Tall trees shielded her from too much sunlight. The soothing murmur of a nearby river danced in her ears.

Half of her mind focused on the soft noises of the world around her and the other half held back, listening to the remains of the eerie silence the forest had left in her.

Madeline felt vulnerable. Her freedom cost her more than she wanted to admit. She had escaped, but to what? Questions flooded her mind, concerns she wished she had thought about before. But before she could plan her future, she needed to take care of today. That meant food, fire, and someplace safe to sleep.

Her stomach growled in agreement. Pushing off the nagging thoughts, she focused on finding the sweet blackberries and thimbleberries that grew in the brambles.

After hours of foraging for berries, she gave up. She had found enough to satisfy her hunger, with a little left over. Red and purple juice stained the bottom of her apron, matching the scattered bruises along her body. Dark shadows underlined her eyes, and her hair had collected itself in one giant tangle. She was a mess. No one would mistake her for a princess now.

If only Sophia could see her, she thought with a chuckle that quickly soured to regret.

Being full did not solve all her problems. The darkness snuck up on her. The hours of berry picking had left little time for her to make a shelter or fire. Before she could do more than lean some fallen branches over a rock, she could hardly see her hands. Without a fire, the darkness engulfed her.

Darkness seemed to escalate the noises of the forest, driving her further under her sticks, closer to the rocks. She hadn't noticed the other sounds before. But now that she was alone, the noises of the wilderness, crunching branches, rustling leaves, chirping birds, coos, and scratches, rushed at her.

Her eyes drooped, weary from the long day. The moment they shut, memories of the brutal attack surfaced. She could clearly hear their screams. Shuddering at the thoughts, she tried to remember the last happy experience she remembered: the tournament. She drifted off to sleep.

She awoke the next day, startled. Birds chirped on the branches above her. Sunlight peeked through several holes in her roof where smaller sticks had fallen away. The morning frost had settled over her, dampening her clothes and feet. Her back itched from the dirt that had settled between her dress and skin. With a loud yawn, she stretched and looked around at her new home. The green trees sparkled with drops of dew, the river bubbled in the background, and soft streams of light shone on and around her. She glanced at the base of the tree where she had hidden her extra berries. Nothing remained. She awoke cold, empty-handed, and confused.

She didn't even have a weapon to protect herself. The dagger, although useful up close, was awkward to handle and did not pose enough of a threat to stop someone, at least not when she used it. She had learned that the hard way.

Looking around the forest, she decided to fix that first. She needed something bigger, something more dangerous. Tying up her tangled mess of hair, she got to work.

The hike to the river was shorter than she had anticipated. Guided by the sound of the waves, she climbed over fallen logs, around rocks, and through soft mud. When she arrived at the river's edge, it exceeded her expectations. A pathway of rocks crossed it at several points. Gentle waves rolled over and around the natural paths in soft ripples. Kneeling down at the edge, she looked at her reflection and smiled. She hardly recognized herself. Except for her telltale green eyes, she looked like a simple village girl.

The cold water refreshed her as she washed her hands and face. Taking a step back, she glanced over the forest and river.

"Aha!" she exclaimed, running to a large oak tree where a forked branch jutted out from the roots. She knelt, grabbing the stick with all her might, feeling the rocks dig into her knees. Pain raced up her legs from all her bruises, but she kept going. She needed to get the stick free. Falling back when it broke, she cried out sharply. Her face crinkled both from pain and surprise.

She grabbed handfuls of rocks, tossing and weighing each in turn. The discarded rocks skipped the surface of the river with a plunk. Looking through the variety of quartz, river rocks, and gravel, she finally settled on a large chunk of slate. Holding her forked stick in one hand and her stone in the other, she got to work.

Ripping a small strip of her apron, she tied the rock into the forked branches of the stick. Once complete, her staff rivaled a knight's club. A crude version, certainly, but workable for what she needed.

Her first swings were awkward. The unbalanced weight threw her off, knocking her over and pulling her behind her swing. But slowly she became comfortable and proficient. For a moment, even with the lack of shelter, food, and fire, she felt secure.

That moment didn't last long. She hiked back to her camp and saw her shelter once more. As she looked at the pile of leaves she had used as a blanket and the sticks that covered her bed, she began to doubt.

Leaning her new club against the tree, she sat down to think. Her fingers struggled with her tangled hair as she turned the ragged mess into a braid. In her mind, she relived previous days.

Her mind spun with images of vivid colors, wondrous cheers, and excitement. She saw the green silk gown her father had given her and the moment of nervousness in his eyes as she twirled around the corner. She also remembered it lying in a heap on her floor, discarded in her act of defiance.

She recalled the ball and the light melody that the musicians had played. The sweet stringing of chords flowed like a river. Couples twirled around the dance floor, oblivious to her tantrums. Honored guests, ignored and mocked by her reaction.

And the tournament, filled with acrobats, knights, mock battles, excitement, and skill. It was an event unlike any other she had seen. She could remember the thumping of horses matching her heartbeat, the thrill she had felt as Sir Daniel moved up the leaderboard, and the warmth of the cheers around her. Painfully, she remembered her long run back to the castle.

All at once, she realized how her own actions had marred the beauty of the memories. How had her stubbornness blocked her from seeing the reasons behind her father's demands?

Madeline sighed deeply. When it came down to it, she had gotten what she had wanted. On her own, in the forest, she had no one to answer to, no demands to follow, and no life choices made without her consent. Here, she had everything she wanted. Why wasn't she happy?

Deep in her heart, she knew the answer. And she knew what she had to do. Grabbing her club, she started back toward the river. She didn't know the way exactly, but she knew the river would lead her to the outskirts of the village.

The smile on her face melted. In the distance, beneath the soft chirping of the birds, a slow rumble grew. Leaning in to the tree, she heard the galloping of hooves coming closer and closer.

"Someone's coming," she said. Holding the club against her chest, feeling the racing of her heart as it throbbed in and out, she waited. Hugging her body against the tree, she closed her eyes and listened as the horse approached her hiding spot.

The rumbling grew to a roar. Her mind raced with images of bandits on horses. She envisioned the burly men who had captured her, the cruel way they had looked at her, and the screams of the village girl. With that image firmly in her mind, she jumped out from behind the tree and swung with all her might.

The club vibrated out of her hands as it connected with the rider. He crashed to the forest floor with a resounding thud.

The thrill of her success disappeared as she looked from the horse to the man. Covered in the red and gold of her kingdom, he looked familiar. She gasped in recognition.

"Sir Daniel," she said, falling to her knees beside him. "Daniel," she whispered, moving his hair out of his eyes.

"Princess," he whispered. "Your eyes…" his voice trailed off to silence.

CHAPTER EIGHTEEN

The sun had begun to set by the time Daniel fully woke up. She had taken them back to her camp. It wasn't improved from her first attempts, but it provided a feeling of security for her. She knelt at his side, flailing her hands in front of his face.

"Are you all right?" she asked when he opened his eyes.

He grimaced as he sat up, clutching at his chest. "I'm all right, just a little surprised." He coughed. She jumped back as he reached for her.

"My princess, I've been looking all over for you."

"I didn't need to be found. I was doing fine on my own," she said.

"Trust me, I can see you were doing all right on your own," he laughed, pointing to the blood on his shirt.

His warm smile melted her irritation.

"Here, have some of these," she offered, holding out a handful of berries she had collected while he slept. "You'll feel better after this and more sleep."

"I feel better just being here with you. I couldn't lose you," Daniel said, looking into her eyes.

His hands rested in hers as he took some of the berries. This time, she didn't move away.

The next day they rode toward the castle. The horse knew the way home, and after hours of meandering through the forest, they reached the lowlands. They saw the castle on the horizon, still in the distance but closer than Madeline had thought.

With each step, she watched the landscape change. The gray castle and colorful banners of her home grew bigger and brighter as they drew closer.

She leaned into Daniel's arms, feeling secure within his embrace. She listened to his stories, laughing about the training practices of the knights and the follies of his youth. The smooth tone of his voice put her at ease.

"You seem familiar to me," she said, squinting back at him.

"Really?" he smiled.

"Are you sure we haven't met before?"

His forehead wrinkled as he thought. "You were at my knighting ceremony," he said.

"Yes, I'm at all of those. Truth be told, they all blend together." She saw his face fall at her words. "The ceremonies blend together, not the knights," she assured him, letting her hand linger on his. "I must have met you somewhere. Around the castle, maybe?"

"I suppose, with our duties, we run in and out all day long. I see you all the time."

"Tell me about it," she said.

"About seeing you?" Daniel looked at her strangely.

"No," she laughed. "Tell me about being a knight. Is it every bit as wonderful as I imagine? The tournaments, journeys, adventure… it all seems so exciting." Her eyes brightened at the romantic notions that had filled her mind since childhood.

He paused to think about it. "Yes and no. There are moments of adventure and moments of triumph, but most of the days are filled with hard work, preparation, and duty."

She cringed at the word *duty*. It seemed like something no one could escape.

"Are those brief moments worth it? Worth all the hard work you put into it? Is a moment of adventure worth a month of ceremonies and routine?"

"Absolutely!" he said. "For a moment, they're worth everything and more. Being a knight is not a dream, but a calling. It's an honor for me and my family."

"You have always wanted to be a knight, and I have always wanted an adventure. You achieved your goal…" her voice trailed off.

He touched her chin and looked her in the eyes. "You've achieved yours too."

"It's not quite the same," she murmured.

"Well, what did you want?"

She thought about it and looked ahead to the castle, watching the banner become clearer and the red dragon more ominous. "I don't know exactly. I suppose this escape was to show my father that I'm not a doll. He can't put me on a shelf to be admired from afar. I want a life to live, to cherish, to love," she whispered, feeling herself blush.

"You deserve all that and more, Princess. I know he just wants the best for you. I mean, when he thought you were dead—"

"What!" Her stomach flipped.

Daniel's words rushed together, explaining the events since she had left.

She didn't wait. Grabbing the reins from Daniel's hands, she kicked the horse into action. She needed to get home and end this charade. The landscape blurred around her as they rushed to the castle.

Before long, cobblestones sounded beneath the horse's hooves, and they were inside the main gates. Leaping off the horse, she flew through the courtyard, ignoring the gasps around her. Up and through the main gates, she ran from room to deserted room, looking for her father. Her torn apron twisted around her as she ran through the narrow corridors.

One of her father's trusted men stood outside the king's chamber.

"Where's my father?" she demanded.

"Princess," the steward's voice wavered. "Is it you?" Tears welled up in his eyes as he stared at her.

She didn't have time to soften the surprise or explain. "The king, where is he?" she growled.

The man, still in shock, pointed down the hall. "He's in your room."

"Thank you!" she yelled, running back down the hall. She dashed up the stairs and around corners, twisting through the darkened halls until she reached her bedroom. Behind the thick wooden door, she heard his sobs. Her heart broke. Placing her palms on the door, Madeline took a deep breath and blinked to keep tears from rolling down her cheeks.

Knocking softly, she waited. When no one answered,

she pushed the door open. Her father sat, hunched over in the chair, contemplating the green dress he had given her for her birthday. His red eyes widened.

"Father," she whispered, closing the door behind her.

King Theodore looked up at her. His face paled, his chin trembling as if he'd seen a ghost. He dropped the green gown and opened his arms. "Madeline?" he choked.

"Father," she wept, folding herself into his arms.

CHAPTER NINETEEN

They sat in silence. The tears lasted for a while at the beginning of their reunion, but soon stopped, leaving four bloodshot eyes as evidence.

Her father's eyes swept over her. "You're home," he said, cupping her face in his hands. There was a smile on his face she hadn't seen in a long time.

"Yes, I'm home. I'm where I belong," she replied, sighing a little but knowing it was true.

"My dear, you had the kingdom quite worried. Prince Paulsen's men brought back your dress. What happened?" he asked, with genuine concern.

She wrinkled her nose at the mention of the prince. "That was an unfortunate consequence. I had a few of those, and none that I am particularly proud of. But I'm home now, and we can forget about the past. I didn't intend for…"

"You did not intend," he mused. "What did you intend by disrespecting me, disobeying me, humiliating me in front of the kingdom, and running away?"

"Yes, I made mistakes. I admit that. But so did you," she countered.

"Well…" he stammered, at a loss for words.

"Yes, you did too. You forgot that, above being a princess, I am your daughter, and I should have more say in my life. Including who and when I marry." She reached for his hands and looked him in the eyes. "I'm here now, and we can fix this."

"You're right. You're home, and none of that other stuff matters now. The most important thing is that you are home, and safe. Everything else can be forgotten with time and with a ceremony."

"With a ceremony? Father, surely you are not still thinking about a marriage at a time like this?"

"Now Madeline, I've heard what you have to say, but it's still your duty," he said, tension crackling in his voice.

"Yes, it's my duty, but it's also supposed to be a joy. Just like the happiness you had with mother. I want that for me. Don't force me to marry someone I don't want. Let me choose."

"You would choose?" he asked.

Her mind raced with pictures of all the suitors and the men of the kingdom and settled onto one in her mind. "Yes, Father, I would."

"Then it's settled. That's an arrangement I can live with." He grasped her hands and pulled her to the chair he had draped the green gown across.

"Do you know why I gave you this dress for your birthday?" he asked. "The first time I met your mother, she wore this. When I saw her enter the room and meet my eyes for the first time, I knew she was meant to be my queen." King Theodore stopped for a moment to hold back his tears. He smiled at her, his eyes distant. "I wanted you to have that same moment of happiness and love in your life."

"I now believe that I will," she said, caressing the soft silk and golden embroidery. "Thank you."

Her father looked at her, waiting for her to continue. "But?"

"But from here on out, we have to make an agreement. I know that I still have a lot to learn, and I need your guidance. But I also have to make some choices and mistakes on my own," she finished, letting out a deep breath of air. She suddenly felt surer of herself and what she was saying.

King Theodore looked down at her and smiled. "It's in moments like this that I see your mother in you. We'll work together," he agreed.

She felt comforted as his velvet robe wrapped around her, in a way she hadn't since she was a child.

CHAPTER TWENTY

The next few weeks were a whirlwind of activity. Once news of her return circulated, there was hardly a corner she could turn or a hallway she could walk down without being bombarded with greetings, smiles, and warm wishes.

During this time, Madeline learned about the agreement her father had made with Prince Paulsen. While she wasn't surprised, she was dismayed to hear about it. Relief was an understatement when she realized how close she had come to being handed over. Going from one captor to another, prince or not, was not her plan.

News had also spread about the new ball and her choosing of a husband. No one wanted to miss it.

On the day of the ball, the castle was in an uproar. Constant deliveries of flowers and food filed through the corridors as the ballroom filled with decorations. The stewards ran from stores to rooms, preparing, cooking, and planning. King Theodore, normally predictable, had surprised them. This ball was planned with specific input from Madeline.

Princess Madeline finished dressing in her room and appraised her image in the mirror. In a matter of weeks, the young girl had transformed into a beautiful woman. She tried to imagine how her mother had looked in the dress.

Fitting her like a glove, the green silk hugged her

body and accentuated her bright eyes. The golden embroidery added a muted elegance and the pearls gleamed in the light. She smiled as she looked at herself in the mirror and felt the fabric roll against her skin. She felt like a queen.

Music and commotion drew her away from the mirror to her window. Looking outside, under the brilliant sunset, she saw sparkling dresses and groups of men crowding toward the door. Visitors and guests overflowed from the ballroom into the courtyard. She listened to the loud bursts of laughter and smiled. Tonight was a night for joy and celebration. She was ready.

After one last look in the mirror, she began the familiar path to the top of the stairway, stopping at the velvet curtain. One of her father's favorite stewards guarded the curtain. She returned his warm smile.

She wasn't sure which scared her more: being captured in the woods or facing a future of choices. Both were daunting in their own way, offering their own adventures. But suddenly, the adventure at the bottom of the stairs seemed enough for her.

The steward who stood guard at the top of the steps was having trouble holding in his smile as she peeked over his shoulders.

"You look beautiful, Princess," he said.

Madeline smiled back and took a deep breath, letting her confidence rise. The butterflies started in her stomach as soon as she heard the trumpets blare. Taking deep breaths, she rubbed her palms over her stomach.

"I can do this," she said, reaching for the handrail.

The trumpets resounded through the hall, announcing her entrance. A moment of stunned silence greeted her as she came into the full view of her father and their guests. The whole hall was quiet, silenced by her beauty before erupting with applause. She had never looked so beautiful, poised, or confident. Radiance surrounded her, and she glowed with every move.

She searched the crowd as she descended the stairs. Her father watched with a look of pride that she hadn't seen in a long time, and Braden stood hand-in-hand with Sophia. She saw some men gathered together, elbowing each other and gawking. The women stopped their chatter and gossip to look at her with visible envy.

Tonight, instead of a crowd of eager suitors, her father greeted her.

After a deep curtsey, she wrapped her arm in his.

"Father," she said with a smile.

His blue eyes beamed with pride. "Are you ready for this?" he asked, covering her hand with his. "You're sure this is the choice you want to make?"

"I have never been so sure of anything," she said with a radiant smile, stepping into position for their first dance.

The music started and Madeline danced with her father, in harmony with him and the music.

"You're so beautiful," he said. "When you came down those stairs, I thought I was seeing a memory. You look exactly like your mother." She saw tears well up in his eyes and gave him a warm smile. He continued, "I saw you, but I also saw the woman you've become. You make me so proud." He held out his arms and twirled her underneath.

Madeline smiled and continued to dance until the final note sounded. As the music stopped, she looked around the hall, feeling the butterflies return. She tried to hide her smile as Braden and Sophia disappeared into a darkened corner. Finally understanding, she laughed.

The music started back up, and a new dance began. Other couples joined in, twirling in harmony with the flutes.

She pressed her way through the crowds, seeing familiar faces intermixed with strangers. The knights from the surrounding territories, healed from the tournament, lined the outer edges of the hall. Soft candlelight reflected off their armor. Her eyes scanned the line but did not stop.

Turning around, she saw Prince Paulsen approach her, creating a wake in the sea of people. Everything about him looked polished, from his black boots to the shine of his hair. His smug smile lacked the charm that had previously impressed her.

"Princess," he began, "would you please honor me with a dance?" he asked, bowing and holding his hand out for her acceptance. "I am sure you heard of my valiant attempts at your rescue," he prodded when she hesitated.

Madeline tried to think of a polite way to decline, and as she looked around for an excuse, someone caught her eye.

"Yes," she stammered, pulling her hand away. "I heard about your attempts. While I respect your valor, I must show my appreciation first to the knight who did not give up hope. Please excuse me," she said, turning away.

As she crossed the ballroom, she glanced back and saw Prince Paulsen's glare.

"I can do this, I can do this," she repeated, trying to quiet the tremors inside her stomach.

Once she saw Daniel, her eyes refused to leave his face. He looked so handsome and regal out of his armor.

Stopping within arm's reach, she curtsied and tapped him on the shoulder.

"Sir Daniel," she said, batting her eyes at him. "I am so glad you could join us this evening." Hoping he couldn't see how fast her heart was beating in her chest, she forced a confident smile to her lips. This was all so new to her.

"Princess," he said, bowing. "You look beautiful."

"Thank you," she said, fighting with her fingers, trying to keep her hands still and at her side. "I've been looking for you."

"You have?" he asked, surprised.

Taking a deep breath, she refocused and smiled. "Yes. You never gave up on me. Even when everyone else thought I was gone," she said, looking away for a second to catch her breath.

Behind his shoulder, she saw a tear twinkle in her father's eyes. No matter what lay ahead, she knew she'd made the right choice.

"Daniel, as my knight champion, it is your duty to follow me, protect me, and make sure that no harm comes to me. While that is the job of a knight, it is also the joy of a husband. Sir Daniel, if you will have me, I choose you." She lowered her gaze and waited, feeling her heart pound

---

out of her chest.

Madeline squealed as he took her in his arms and squeezed her tight.

"It would be my honor and privilege," he said, lifting her fingers to his lips. "I've wanted to give you this." He placed something smooth in her hand. "I found it as I was searching for you. It reminded me of your eyes and gave me hope."

Cupped in her hands was a polished green shell, round and scaled, flawless.

"It's beautiful," she said, turning the shell over in her hands, watching a rainbow reflect off its ridges.

"Not nearly as beautiful as you."

Madeline smiled as Daniel lifted his hand to her face and leaned forward for a tender kiss. Looking at each other, they barely heard the music start a new dance. He held her in his arms and both were oblivious to everything around them.

EPILOGUE

Standing in a semi-circle on the shore of the lake, the wizards gazed into the depths of the mirror. Elias knelt in the water, letting the magic of the mirror cover him. The hairs on the back of his neck prickled with energy. Behind him, a quiet hum reverberated from their chant.

The lake's surface filled with colors that both matched and contrasted with the sunset above. The collage of light and shadows swirled to create an image. The pictures formed clearly, and he smiled. Sir Daniel had found his princess after all.

"Perfect," he said, moving to the shoreline. The scene in the water settled into faded ripples, and the images of Daniel and Madeline blurred until the water was smooth again. A smile filled his face, knowing they were back on track.

"Eleanor, your daughter has finally come into her own. Your sacrifice was not for nothing." He clapped his hands together and addressed the wizards around him.

"Fellow wizards, it has begun. The time for action draws near. We must prepare for the changes to come. We will be needed."

A line of green robes followed him as he walked up the steep trail leading from the shoreline back into the mountains. Their robes sparkled in the moonlight.

ABOUT THE AUTHOR

Kirstin Pulioff is a storyteller at heart. Born and raised in Southern California, she moved to the Pacific Northwest to follow her dreams and graduated from Oregon State University with a degree in Forest Management. Happily married and a mother of two, she lives in the foothills of Colorado. When she's not writing an adventure, she's busy living one.

Website: www.kirstinpulioff.com
Facebook: KirstinPulioffAuthor
Twitter: @KirstinPulioff

Published Works
Middle Grade Fantasy
    The Escape of Princess Madeline
    The Battle for Princess Madeline
    The Dragon and Princess Madeline

    The Princess Madeline Trilogy (box set)
YA Fantasy
    Dreamscape: Saving Alex
Short Stories
    The Ivory Tower
    Boone's Journey

THE BATTLE FOR PRINCESS MADELINE
(Book Two of the Princess Madeline series)

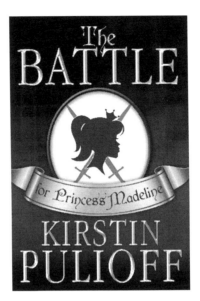

Princess Madeline rejected Prince Paulsen's advances, but he's not about to take it lying down. In the middle of Soron's festival preparations, when his obsession jeopardizes the kingdom, mysterious figures from the past arrive. Can Madeline risk accepting their help or will their information about a family secret be too much for her to handle?

Can Madeline trust anyone or will saving the kingdom come down to her own bravery?

Available in digital and print formats from most online distributors.

THE DRAGON AND PRINCESS MADELINE
(Book Three of the Princess Madeline series)

Princess Madeline is ready to celebrate. With the foundation of her future in place, it seems nothing can hurt her. Then the return of a mysterious green dragon threatens their kingdom and king. Will this challenge prove to be too much for Princess Madeline and Prince Braden or will they find the answers they seek hidden in cryptic messages from the past?

Can Madeline save her kingdom from the dragon or is the real danger something else?

Available in digital and print formats from most online distributors.

Made in the USA
Middletown, DE
09 December 2015